Advance Praise

"A captivating, beautifully written novel about passion and exile, devoted siblings and new lovers, and the unifying enchantment of music. The exquisitely human, bighearted characters of *The Deceived Ones* will stay with you long after you read the last page."

— Jane Delury, author of *Hedge* and *The Balcony*

"*The Deceived Ones* is a delightful homage to *Twelfth Night* and the latest literary triumph from Judith Krummeck, who effortlessly weaves a romantic tale abounding with art, geopolitics, and contemporary life in all its tragic, beautiful glory."

— Ben Tanzer, author of *UPSTATE, Orphans,* and *Be Cool*

"Judith Krummeck has taken the charming, soulful plot of *Twelfth Night* and transformed it into a believably contemporary story, immersing it in the fascinating backdrop of premier classical music and composition. As a Shakespeare lover, while I knew the outlines of the plot, I delighted in the journey, the adaptation of the story, and the choices the author made in getting us there. An enjoyable twist on a familiar tale and a compelling take on a world I didn't know."

— Lesley Malin, Producing Executive Director, Chesapeake Shakespeare Company

"A moving yet understated novel of love and loss, international politics, and the timeless power of music, *The Deceived Ones*, like a great song, demands our attention right now . . . "

> — Betsy Boyd, author and program director, M.F.A. in Creative Writing & Publishing Arts, University of Baltimore

"With exquisite prose and unforgettable characters, Judith Krummeck's debut novel, *The Deceived Ones*, offers a multifaceted look at love, loss, longing—and the power of human connection. In the wake of the humanitarian crisis caused by Russia's invasion of Ukraine, this novel entangles such themes as migration, adaptation, deception, sexuality, diversity, human connection, and the influence of music as a universal language. Don't be deceived: this novel will pluck your heartstrings and have you humming its inspired tune long after you turn the final page."

> — Eric D. Goodman, author of *Tracks: A Novel in Stories* and *Setting the Family Free*

The Deceived Ones

Judith Krummeck

Apprentice
House Press
Loyola University Maryland

First Edition

Library of Congress Control Number: requested

Hardcover ISBN: 978-1-62720-528-3
Paperback ISBN: 978-1-62720-529-0
Ebook ISBN: 978-1-62720-530-6

Cover Design by Apprentice House Press
Design Editing by Claire Marino
Promotional Development by Maddie Holmes
Editorial Development by Abby McLeod
Cover image of Baltimore Skyline by Yurkaimmortal via VectorStock.com
Cover image of viola da gamba courtesy of The Met under Creative Commons
Zero (CC0) license

Published by Apprentice House Press

Apprentice
House Press
Loyola University Maryland

Loyola University Maryland
4501 N. Charles Street, Baltimore, MD 21210
410.617.5265
www.ApprenticeHouse.com
info@ApprenticeHouse.com

To Peter, my twin in all but age

To the people of Ukraine and their courage to be

What country, friends, is this?
— *Shakespeare, Twelfth Night, Act 1, Scene 2*

If music be the food of love, play on …
— *Shakespeare, Twelfth Night, Act 1, Scene 1*

PROLOGUE

THE TRAIN JERKS AND BEGINS TO MOVE FORWARD, but Vira keeps her hand pressed against the window, where her palm is separated from Sevastyan's by the pane of glass. He has his cell phone to his ear and she to hers.

"It's okay," he says, walking alongside the moving train, "It will not be long."

How can he say that? He has no idea what will happen. Neither has she.

The train picks up speed, and their palms pull apart. He stands still, dropping his hand to his side. She keeps her eyes fixed on him in the midst of the seething crowd under the Art Nouveau dome of the platform at the Lviv-Holovnyi railway station, the chaos a microcosm of the country, the scene receding as the train gathers momentum.

Sevastyan ... Sevastyan ... she hears his name in the rhythm of the wheels on the tracks. She can no longer make him out in the throng of the crowd, but she keeps staring and searching. Then the train station disappears from view.

"Goodbye, Sobka," she says.

"Goodbye, Vironka," he says.

She stares down at the screen of her phone, not wanting to click on the red X, but then Sevastyan ends the call. *Sevastyan ... Sevastyan ...* clacks the rhythm of the wheels, carrying her further and further away from him.

"That was your brother, I think?"

She realizes that the old man sitting opposite is speaking to her.

She nods. "My twin."

"Ah! A remarkable likeness."

She is used to this. People are always commenting on how much she and Sevastyan look alike; the same high cheekbones, straight black hair, green eyes.

She looks away from the old man, glancing around the over-crowded train compartment, and then out of the window. They are traveling west, following the sun towards the border. She pulls a face-mask from her coat pocket and puts it on, holding herself in self-contained silence. She so desperately doesn't want to be on this train with a horde of strangers, to be leaving without Sevastyan. She'd wavered and waited—even as the calls became more imperative for women, children, and the elderly to leave while they could—hoping until the last minute that he would still be able to come with her. But when the war started, no men of conscription age could leave Ukraine.

Held between her feet is her backpack with toiletries, two changes of underwear, a few T-shirts, another pair of shoes, one tightly rolled dress, along with her passport and other essential documents. She's wearing all the bulky things—coat, jersey, scarf, hat, boots—and she has brought as little as possible so that she can also carry her precious instrument.

"Is that a cello?" the old man asks.

"It's a viola da gamba."

She is expecting to have to explain it, as usual, and though she doesn't want to be rude, she can't face making polite conversation with this stranger.

But he nods and says, "Ah! Marin Marais."

She takes proper note of him for the first time then. Very few people can name that master of the viol. "How do you know about Marin Marais?"

"I like, very much, the music of the Renaissance and the Baroque," he says. "When it gets to Mozart and Beethoven, it is too modern for me."

They share a half laugh, oddly out of place in the circumstances, then they lapse into silence again.

Where is Sevastyan now, Vira wonders. On his way back to their flat? *Sevastyan ... Sevastyan ...* goes the rhythm of the wheels.

After a time, the old man says, "Your heart is breaking to leave your twin."

His empathy gives her a stab of regret for trying to shut him out. She doesn't trust herself to speak in case even one word causes the dam wall of held-in tears to burst.

"Will you and your viola da gamba, meanwhile, make a new home in Poland?"

She looks him full in the face. He must be in his eighties, yet there is something vigorous in him. His face is broad, and his abundant white hair, receding just at the temples, spirals into loose coils. She feels an odd intimacy being encased in a train hurtling towards the Poland border, sitting opposite this old stranger whom she will never see again once this desperate journey is over.

"Maybe I will stay there for now," she says, "but perhaps..." She trails off, not knowing how to articulate something that is only a blurred illusion in her own mind. Yet she senses that she could say things to this old man in their weird cocoon of transience that it would be hard to share if the circumstances weren't so outside the ordinary. She says, "Before the invasion, I used to dream about studying viol in America. It is just a fantasy. It is impossible, but ..."

The old man's pale blue eyes almost disappear into wrinkles as he smiles. "If you do not dream, then you do not know what you want, and then you can never grasp your fantasy."

"When I get to Krakow," she says, "perhaps I can try to find a way."

"You know how our old Ukrainian proverb goes: 'Luck always seems to be against the man who depends on it.' But you are young," he says. "You do not have to depend on luck. You have time to make your own."

"And you?" she asks. "Will you stay in Poland?"

"I have a cousin in Warsaw who says he will take me in. But I hope it will not be long before I can go back home. I am too old to start a new life."

A child gives a sharp cry, cutting through the rumbling murmur of the crowd packed into the train compartment, and Vira looks towards the sound before it is shushed. The faces all around her are stretched blank, as if to cordon off the anxiety and dislocation inside.

VIRA

IT IS SIX MONTHS LATER when Vira walks into the arrivals hall at Baltimore Washington International Thurgood Marshall Airport. She scans the crowd waiting there, and her eyes stop at a sign that reads *Vira Blyzinskyj* in both Latin and Cyrillic alphabets. It is held by a tall, wiry woman with spiky gray hair. She's wearing a face mask, as is Vira.

The woman moves towards her. "Vira?" she asks.

"Yes," she says.

"I'm Peta Masters."

"I am glad to meet you," says Vira, holding her instrument case in both hands to avoid the awkwardness of whether or not to shake hands in a world still on edge about COVID-19.

Peta folds the sign and stuffs it into her crossbody bag as she says, "Ласкаво просимо до Америки!" to welcome Vira to America.

"Ви говорите моєю мовою!" Vira is taken aback that an American speaks her language.

"I speak very little, I'm afraid," Peta says, reverting to English. "My grandfather was from Ukraine, and he taught me a word here and there." She gestures towards Vira's backpack and instrument case. "Do you have more bags to collect?"

"No."

"Come, then. Let's get you home. Can I carry anything?"

"No, thank you. I am fine."

As they walk towards the parking garage Peta asks, "How was your flight?"

"Long!" Vira expels her breath on a dry laugh, and her mask puffs out. She feels jittery and disoriented with exhaustion. "From Krakow, to Munich, then Chicago, then here."

"Did you fly to Krakow from Ukraine?"

"No, I took train. It is seven hours from Lviv to Krakow. I stayed there many months to find if I can come here."

Peta pops the trunk of a Prius. "Well, it's just one more car ride before the end of your long journey," she says. "We'll have you home and in bed before midnight."

With great care, Vira places her instrument case in the trunk, keeping her backpack with her as she climbs into the passenger seat. At least driving on the right is one thing that is that same as in Ukraine.

As Peta cranes her head to reverse out of the parking space she asks, "How did you hear about the Uniting for Ukraine program?"

"At Ukrainian consulate in Krakow," says Vira. "They said it is for people to bring their family to America. But then there was your name, for anybody who needs help."

Peta follows a sign that reads *Balt Wash Pkwy,* heading north. She says, "I wanted to try to help someone partly because of my grandfather. I live in his old house near Patterson Park, and there's a strong Ukrainian community around there."

Vira turns to her in astonishment. "I did not know this," she says.

"My grandfather came here after World War Two," says Peta, "the last time there was a refugee crisis on this scale. But Ukrainians have been settling in the Baltimore area since the nineteenth century." She flicks on her indicator to change lanes. "There's a beautiful gold-domed Ukrainian Catholic church just across from Patterson Park, and the community has a festival every September with music and dancing and food."

"How many Ukrainians live there?" asks Vira.

"I'd guess maybe about five hundred. More will likely come now."

Vira nods, staring ahead through the windshield. She texts daily with Sevastyan via the Telegram app, terrified for his safety and heartbroken for their battered country. Even though the Russians have not been able to capture Kyiv—yet—the devastation and dislocation are unthinkable. As proud as she is of President Volodymyr Zelenskyy and her people, she can't bear to think at what cost.

PETA

WHAT MUST SHE BE FEELING? Peta wonders. Leaving her country, and most likely friends and family; traveling all on her own to a strange country; having to deal with all the paperwork and bureaucracy; being dependent on strangers ... and all in a foreign language. Peta tries to intuit whether she should just leave Vira with her thoughts, or continue trying to draw her out. She's been immediately drawn to this slender, striking young woman, who emanates an aura of vulnerability, grace, and grit.

When Russia invaded Ukraine, Peta's horror at the unfolding human tragedy and resultant displacement galvanized her into searching for ways to help. The moment she heard about the Uniting for Ukraine program, she submitted an online application, answering the questions about her income, household size, the number of individuals she wished to sponsor, and federal poverty guidelines. She could only afford to take in one refugee, not a family, but it was better than nothing, she thought. She underwent the background check and completed the mandatory training, throwing herself into the process as much to try and bring some structure to her life as to be of service.

She'd offered to take Vira into her now-hollow home in the hopes that the comings and goings of another person might help to give some shape to her amorphous days. She's felt unmoored, floundering around in a tangle of unpredictable emotions, since Julie's death last year. After observing the official period of mourning allowed after the loss of a spouse, she'd tried to return to the familiar rhythm of her work at the Institute of Marine and Environmental Technology. But it was impossible to find a pattern in the vacuum of what had been. For eighteen years, she'd shared every detail of her research, her setbacks, her daily joys, with her wife. Now, her work and life seem pointless. There is no joy. Her days are endless. Her nights even longer. She'd cast about, trying to find something, anything, that could give her life some meaning.

She pulls her mind away from these thoughts and concentrates on the present.

"Do you have family still in Ukraine?" she asks.

"Yes, my brother," says Vira. "No man between eighteen and sixty may leave."

"Oh, that's so hard!"

Peta glances over at Vira's set face. The tragedy of it all is so overwhelming that she can't think of anything to say that won't sound banal. And if she feels this way, she can't imagine what it must be like to live it. That feeling of displacement is unfathomable.

"I did not want to leave," Vira says, "to come on my own..." and her voice catches on the last phrase.

ORSON

ORSON PLAYS THE PHRASE AGAIN, modulating to a minor key, and he likes the way the plaintive quality adds depth and texture to the melody line. But when he tries to develop the theme, the tonality doesn't work anymore. He bangs a discord on the piano and drops his hands from the keyboard. It's been like this all day. He thinks he's getting somewhere, and then it all falls apart.

He stretches his neck to one side and then the other, trying to ease the tension. He plucks the damp T-shirt away from his skin. His old rowhouse, charming as it is, has no air conditioning, and the ceiling fan is no match for the stultifying humidity of a Baltimore summer.

Every part of him is straining to give up, get up, and walk away. But he can't. Every second that he isn't composing brings the implacable deadline closer. When the commission initially came through from the Twelfth Night Festival, he felt as if he had all the time in the world. But now, January is perilously close. Pre-production on the opera will have to be in full swing in three months—at the very latest. Curtis is on his case daily because the designers are hounding *him* for a concept, while the Festival marketing department is hounding the designers. The domino effect always cycles back to Orson being under pressure to deliver.

Orson fingers the keyboard, trying out the modulation from the major to the minor again. He shifts down a key, experimenting. It still doesn't have the quality he's after. How can this be so damned difficult? It's always come so intuitively before. *Think of the context!* He directs himself. Olivia is mourning the death of her brother; shielding herself from society in her grief. Her aria has to be in a minor key. He stares off into a corner of the room, one segment of his mind registering a cobweb there while he tries to conjure the most plaintive key. The ending of Tchaikovsky's *Pathétique Symphony* in B minor comes to mind. He tries out the phrase in that key. Better, but still not quite right. What about B minor's relative, D major? *No!* That doesn't work at all.

With his perfect pitch, he hears in his mind's ear the inimitable voice of Isabella Foiani, who will be singing the role of Olivia. It's a warm, supple instrument, with honey overtones and the clarity of a boy treble. Though she'd started out as a piano major with the same professor as Orson, after a year she'd switched to a concentration in singing. Around the same time, she asked Orson to help her with a musical arrangement for an old Native American song. He became so intrigued by the challenge of marrying a purely handed down oral tradition with notated western music that he ended up doing most of the composing.

His fascination hadn't been only for the music—he was also intensely, unnervingly compelled by Isabella as a woman. With an African American mother and a north Italian father, the combination in Isabella was riveting—gray eyes and a cloud of black hair offsetting a lustrous skin tone that made him think of a finely polished violin. Her beauty was so intimidating that Orson, against every inclination, had kept his distance.

He snaps his mind back from his daydream. *Just think of the voice!* He feels out a melodic line, moving his hand exploratively, intuitively over the keys. The first phrase works. Then it sticks.

His cell phone beeps and he snatches it up, grateful for any distraction, though typically the disruption would infuriate him. He glances at the screen—it's Curtis.

Curtis's smile in his profile picture is just the same as the one that he had presented to Orson when he'd introduced himself, out of the blue, in the Peabody cafeteria almost ten years ago. With winning charm he'd persuaded Orson to write the music for a multimedia presentation that he and Isabella were working on around Elizabeth Alexander's poem, *The Venus Hottentot*—an excoriating take on the colonial objectification of a woman from the ancient San tribe in Southern Africa. With Curtis's energy driving the project, it not only got off the ground but jumped off in myriad unexpected directions, and the shape of Orson's days changed dramatically. Instead of practicing piano for eight hours a day, he was now doing just enough to keep his technique where it needed to be. He spent the rest of his time at the keyboard experimenting with the interweaving, polyphonic chants of the ancient San peoples, working and reworking, so that the musical lines would help, not hurt, Alexander's poetry.

In the end, the response to the production was astounding. It was written up in the papers and online; an agent approached Isabella to represent her; it was videotaped and went viral on YouTube and social media. A small indie label made an audio recording of the production and it went on to win the Discovery

Award at the International Classical Music Awards.

All this seems beyond belief now, when he can't seem to write a single phrase of music.

Curtis's text reads: "Finally got an email from Isabella's assistant."

"Great!" Orson texts back.

"No, not great."

Orson responds with the double exclamation point Tapback, and he watches, impatient, Curtis's three-dot 'writing' symbol.

Curtis texts, "He says Isabella is withdrawing from all public performances for the foreseeable future."

"What?!" Orson almost inserts an anguished emoji, but the situation is too serious for that.

"Withdrawing for personal reasons is what he says."

"Why?!"

"Trying to find out. Will get back to you."

Curtis signs off and Orson stares down at the blank screen, his mind equally blank with the shock of this completely disastrous development. He can't get his head around it. He and Curtis had taken it for granted that Isabella would sing the role of Olivia after they'd all collaborated so well on the *Venus Hottentot* project. This would be their first time working together again, and when Curtis had floated the idea past Isabella, she'd seemed interested. Now, this. *I can't get the music down, and at this rate I'm not even going to have a soprano to sing it!* Orson frets.

He looks at his scrambled notations on the music rack. He tries to focus, to pick up where he left off with Olivia's melody line, but his mind keeps gravitating back to Isabella. She's always been elusive and inscrutable. He remembers the time he was working on a particular segment of *The Venus Hottentot* and she came down to the rabbit warren of practice rooms to find him. She sat on the piano bench next to him, her woody perfume wafting with her, and she sight-read the vocal line he had written.

"Oh my God, you're so good at this, Orson!" she said. "It's exquisite. The dissonance, and this rotating vocal line you write above it—you've completely captured the stark words."

It was difficult to concentrate with her in such close proximity. "If you think the vocal line is working then," he said, "I'll make a start on the instrumentation."

"It's more than working, Orson, it's really great! Thank you."

She'd turned to him on the piano bench, her face alight, looking so vivid and so beautiful that he had to fight a fierce impulse to pull her body against him, put his mouth against her neck, inhale her scent. Instead, he'd stood up abruptly and paced to the furthest corner of the small room.

He turned to face her. "Isabella. You must know how I feel about y—"

"Don't say it," she interrupted, but she said it gently, and her eyes were soft. "Come, let's go and get a drink. We'll see if Curtis is free to join us."

And that's how it was—his hopeless infatuation with her, and her keeping him at arm's length. She'd be warm and effusive one moment, then remote and disengaged the next. The more the *Venus Hottentot* project advanced, the more they were thrown into each other's company, but the tension of that dynamic between them never changed. And now, it seems they're embarked on the same dance.

The soprano *has* to be Isabella! All the time he's been wrestling with writing this opera, he's had the imprint of her unique, velvety voice in his mind. He's composed for her exact timbre and musicality. Nobody else can possibly do it justice. What if she *really* won't do it? The thought makes him stand up abruptly from the piano

14

bench, and he goes over to one of the tall front windows of the room.

There are just one dog walker and a Johns Hopkins student with a backpack out on St. Paul's Street in the humid afternoon heat, and he stares out at them unseeing. When Orson had received the commission from the Twelfth Night Festival, they were all still basking in the astounding win of the Discovery Award, and he'd thought, *if that award was possible, anything is.* Everything leading up to it had felt like a haphazard, improvised experiment—a lark— and the upshot for Orson was that he changed his concentration from piano to composition. He carried the no-holds-barred collective inventiveness of *The Venus Hottentot* into his doctoral degree, culminating in his thesis on the blending of western and indigenous music. He had so much creative energy that he felt as if he would never be able to realize all the ideas jostling for space in his mind.

But this is his first commission. Now, he's being put on the spot to come up with some exceptional piece that he is expected to create to order. The swift trajectory that led to the award for *The Venus Hottentot* had unfolded so seamlessly that it was as if it hadn't really happened to him, as if he was a bystander to someone else's marvelous success. He's acutely aware of the weight of follow-up expectation weighing on him, and he has edgy misgivings that it was all just a fluke. *Am I a fake,* he wonders, *and is everyone about to find that out?* He feels like the embodiment of impostor syndrome. All the music that had been pent up inside him, and had forced its way out in a torrent of creativity, seems now to have evaporated. He is too self-conscious, too over-aware, trying too hard to capture some elusive spark.

He pulls his gaze from the window and looks about him. His music room, which in a typical home would be the living room, is a shambles of music scores and coffee mugs and random bits of discarded clothing.

"What a mess!" he says, whether about the room or the situation he doesn't quite know.

He draws in a deep breath, feeling overwhelmed by the trivia and trauma of it all. Knowing he'll never get any useful work done in this frame of mind, he turns his back on it and walks from the room.

VIRA

WHEN VIRA LEAVES the international rescue committee, she has more of a glimmer of hope than she's allowed herself to feel for months. In the pocket of her dress is the business card of Fariba Mehta. Piece by piece, she's building the small circle of people she knows in this strange American city.

Meticulously, she retraces her steps for the seven-minute walk to the bus stop for the southbound Purple Line of the Charm City Circulator, as instructed by Peta. A few steps from the stop, she sees the bus approaching and runs the last few paces to catch it. It's a relief to take a seat in the air-conditioned comfort of the bus after her spurt of energy in the cloying heat outside. She slips on her face mask and instinctively reaches for the phone in her backpack to send a Telegram text to Sevastyan. She finds two messages from him waiting for her.

"Power out. Phone running low. Must find charging station."

And, sent earlier, "Military medical commission says unfit to serve in military!"

Vira stares down at her phone trying to make sense of the influx of information. She imagines him in Lviv, going in search of one of the solar-powered charging stations that have become a lifeline in the chaos. It's after midnight there already, but the days and nights have blurred with the invasion.

Military medical commission says unfit to serve in military. What does this mean? Her thumbs fly across the screen of her phone as she taps out questions to him. She gets no answer. Either he's asleep or his phone is out of battery. She hates being out of touch with him, even for a few hours. She feels dislocated from what is going on back home—the power outages, the confusion, the terror, the escalating destruction of it all. When she sees it on the news, it's difficult to relate the chaos and devastation to her own country.

She looks up from her phone, knowing that no amount of try-ing to coax an answer from it will make it happen. She takes stock of her surroundings. The bus is approaching a Beaux-Arts building on her right, set at a slight angle to the road, and she turns around in her seat to study it as the bus passes. It appears to be a railway station, and she thinks back to seeing Sevastyan slowly disappear-ing in the throng on the platform of the Lviv-Holovnyi railway sta-tion. The bus continues south past row houses that remind Vira of certain areas of Lviv, and then it comes to a small park on the right. She looks up the incline towards a tall Doric column with a statue mounted on top. Vira's first impressions of Baltimore are that it's a relatively old city—though not compared to Lviv's 13th century origins—with charm, but also neglect and dereliction in some parts.

As the City Circulator approaches Pratt Street at the Inner

Harbor, Vira studies the map to double check that this is where she must change to the Orange line heading east towards Patterson Park. She manages the change without a hitch, and, once inside the cool air conditioning again, she slips her hand into her pocket to finger the business card, making sure that it is still there, taking comfort from it as if it were a talisman. Its owner was small in stature, with the burnished skin of a southern Indian, and a way of smiling with her eyes that made them look like dark, liquid pools.

Fariba had trailed a faint fragrance of patchouli when she led Vira to a small office crammed with mismatched furniture—the leftovers from other bureaucratic offices. There, Vira had shown Fariba her papers—her Ukrainian passport with its student visa stamp, her background check and letters of reference, her medical exemption, and her academic qualifications.

"Are you on your own?" Fariba asked.

"Yes," said Vira, the constant undercurrent of longing and worry breaking to the surface again. "My brother is in Ukraine, waiting and hoping to come."

"It's a heart-breaking time for your country."

Vira was caught off guard by Fariba's empathy, and felt a sudden lump in her throat.

As if to protect Vira from her own vulnerability, Fariba became all business. "Well, let's see what we can do for you. Have you found somewhere to live?"

Vira explained about the Uniting for Ukraine Program, and that she was staying with Peta for now.

"Ah yes, I've heard of that program," said Fariba. "It's sanctioned by the U.S. State Department. Those kinds of volunteer programs are invaluable as we deal with the thousands of refugees that are coming in."

"Ukrainians?" Vira wondered.

"No, you're my first. But the displacement is already a global refugee crisis, and I'm sure we'll see more soon enough."

Vira felt a sense of living history in a ghastly way, of being one fragment of a huge statistic.

"Anyway, it's really great that you've got somewhere to stay," said Fariba. "Housing is hard. Jobs are easier. We also try to help with things like basic public benefits, food stamps, and things like that."

"Please, can you help me find a job?"

"Just so you know, we generally start people out with a survival job in service industries like healthcare, or housekeeping, or food."

"Thank you, this will be fine." She'd done some waitressing as a student.

"Your English is good, so that's going to make things a lot easier for you," Fariba said.

She turned towards the computer on her desk, and Vira watched her dark luminous eyes skim the screen as she scrolled.

"This might be something," Fariba said, glancing again at the copy on her desk of Vira's academic certificate from the Lviv Conservatory. "There's a summer housekeeping position at the Peabody Conservatory. You wouldn't be using your music qualification, of course, but at least you'd be in that environment."

"This would be convenient," Vira responded, even as she had wondered if 'convenient' was quite the right word.

"Okay then, I'll put in an application for you. If it comes through us, you'll be sure to get it."

Fariba had gone off to make copies of Vira's documents before sending her on her way with a promise to get back to her about the job at Peabody as soon as she heard anything.

Now, as the Charm City Circulator angles south, travels east again for a few blocks, and then heads north to the Bank Street stop, Vira shifts to the edge of her seat, pulls on her backpack, and prepares to get off to walk the rest of the way towards Patterson Park. As she steps off the bus, she removes her face-mask, glad to breath air that isn't from her own exhalation. It's after 6 PM by now, the lull between the end of the working day and the start of nightlife. She crosses Broadway, with the strangely asymmetrical towers of a gothic-styled stone church looming over her, and continues walking east alongside Formstone buildings, brick row houses, and shuttered shops. A Roman Catholic church comes up on her right—the city seems to have a church on nearly every block—and she can see the park up ahead where she will turn right to get to Peta's rowhouse.

When the hand is clamped over her mouth, she is caught completely off guard. Her shoulders are violently wrenched, there's a searing slash of pain on her arm, and she is shoved forward with such force that she crashes to her knees on the sidewalk. She staggers to her feet. But, still off balance, she can't fight back when she is lifted and dragged sideways towards a small cross street. She grabs at the hand to try and wrench it away from her mouth as she screams, but the sound is trapped in her throat and mouth. The hand smells of cigarettes. The breath on the side of her face stinks of onions. She gags. As she is dragged, one of her shoes comes off.

She's thrown back against a wall with such force that her head cracks against the mortar. Her scream is cut off as the hand is clamped over her mouth again. She is tall, and her eyes are on a level with her attacker. She writhes and twists, pounding against him, grappling with his other hand as it snakes under her dress. Something tears. She arches and kicks, jerking her head from side to side and struggling to break free as they wrestle in grim silence.

A car shoots past down Bank Street, its windows down, rap music blaring in doppler effect. For a split-second the hand goes slack, and Vira wrenches away towards the street. He grabs at her but she writhes away, kicking off her other shoe, plunging from fight to flight. She is at the corner. She sprints down the row of houses, unmindful of the jagged paving on her bare feet. She is on the steps of Peta's rowhouse. She reaches for her backpack to get the front door key. Her backpack is gone.

She spins around, convinced that he is right behind her, but the street is deserted. A sharp pain in her upper arm makes her look down at it. Blood is oozing from a deep gash. The combination of the sight of her own blood and the catastrophe of what has happened is so overwhelming that a wave of nausea passes through her, and she has to put her hand on the wall of the house to steady herself. Her backpack is gone—and with it her vital documents and her phone. "Мій телефон!" she cries. Her phone is her lifeline to Sevastyan. When he tries to text her again, he won't be able to reach her. Panic laps at her. She leans her forehead against the door, tears starting to stream down her face, and she thumps on the door to be let in.

PETA

SITTING AT THE KITCHEN TABLE, Peta is applying for a research grant on her laptop, but her mind isn't fully on it. She'd expected Vira to return over an hour ago, and she can't settle to her work as the minutes continue to tick by. Gradually, she becomes aware of a soft, rhythmic thumping on the front door.

She scrapes back the kitchen chair and walks through to the entrance hall to peer through the window by the door. She sees Vira's long dark hair falling forward across her shoulder as she leans against the door. When Peta opens the door, Vira looks at her through the curtain of her hair, her face wet with tears.

Alarm shoots through Peta as she reaches to pull Vira inside. "What is it?" she asks. "What's happened?"

A sob seems to force its way out of Vira, her cries erupting so intensely that she can hardly take a breath. Peta's instinct is to wrap her arms around her, but there is something so violent about this distress that she holds back, feeling a little wisp of fear. Tentatively, she takes Vira's hand, peering anxiously into her face, completely at a loss as to what can have happened or how to comfort her. The crisis of Vira's raw crying peaks, and then gradually begins to subside, the two of them standing in the dim hallway, quite still, like a suspended tableau.

Then Vira pulls her hand away from Peta's grasp and smears both hands across her wet cheeks. "I must make phone call," she says, her voice husky. "Please, may I use your phone?"

"Of course!" Peta knows that Vira has her own phone, but this is not the time to question why she doesn't use it. "Come into the kitchen and I'll make you some chamomile tea while you call."

In the light of the kitchen, Peta takes in Vira's bare feet, grazed knees, and a bloody slash across her right arm.

"My God!" exclaims Peta. "We must get those cleaned up."

She pulls out a chair from the table, and Vira sits down abruptly, as if her legs won't hold her any longer. "Please, I must call first."

When Vira sits down, Peta sees that there is blood matted into her hair at the crown of her head. If it were up to her, she would tend to these injuries first, but this is not her emergency; she must try to trust Vira's sense of timing. She keys in the code on her phone and puts it on the table. "Here you are," she says.

Methodically, as if she has to consider every movement, Vira puts a hand into the pocket of her dress, takes out a business card, and dials the number. When it begins to ring, Peta turns away and busies herself getting the tea ready, trying to give Vira some privacy. Behind her, Peta hears Vira draw in a shaky breath over the faint dialing tone. Then the call is picked at the other end.

"I'm sorry—" says Vira.

Peta hears the muffled response on the line.

"It is Vira Blyzinskyj." Her voice is tight and breathless. "I'm sorry, you said I could call you, and I did not know what else to do."

Peta makes out what seems to be a question on the other end of the phone.

"I ..." Vira's breath seems to catch in her throat.

Another question, more urgent this time.

A sob, like a cough, escapes Vira. Trying to speak through her crying, her voice low and guttural, she says, "I was attacked. After I left you. By a man. I lost everything. My phone, my documents, everything—"

Peta feels a jolt of shock. And, with it, guilt. She'd had an all-day meeting at the marine institute today, and had urged Vira to go to the immigrant and refugee center as soon as possible, giving her meticulous instructions about how to use the Charm City Circulator to get there and back. But, if she had taken her, this wouldn't have happened. Peta abandons any pretense of giving Vira privacy, and comes to stand by her, pulling a tissue from the box on the kitchen counter and offering it to her.

"Were you raped?" The voice on the phone is more distinct now.

"No, I ran away, but I lost everything."

"But I have copies of your documents, remember? I took copies of them all."

"Yes. This is why I am calling you."

"Good. Now, this is what I need you to do," the voice goes on. "You must report this to the police. Can you do that?"

"Yes, I will do that," says Vira.

"Then, tomorrow morning, first thing, come into the offices here, and I will give you duplicates of the copies that I made. That way you won't be undocumented. Okay?"

"Yes," says Vira again.

"Where did it happen?"

"Bank Street, when I was walking from circulator bus." She closes her eyes as if visualizing the location.

"Where are you now? Somewhere safe?"

Vira tilts her face up to Peta, her green eyes magnified through tears. "I am with the person from the Uniting for Ukraine program."

"That's good. So, get that police report now, and bring it with you when you come in tomorrow morning, okay?"

"I will. Thank you." Vira disconnects and carefully wipes the cell phone on her dress before putting it down on the table.

Peta says, "Vira, I'm so, *so* sorry. I should have canceled my meeting and come with you."

"This is not your fault."

But Peta believes it is. She has taken this person in and pledged to sponsor her. If she couldn't have canceled her meeting today, she should rather have advised Vira to wait a day and gone with her to the International Rescue Committee. The kettle whistles on the stove, and Peta pours water over the chamomile flowers in the teapot, adding a sprig of mint.

One constructive thing she can do now, at least, is to call the police. She hugs the phone between her shoulder and her ear, pouring the tea into two china cups as she makes the arrangements for the police to come. When she sits down at the table, she watches Vira over the rim of her cup as she blows on the tea to cool it. Vira's beautiful face is blotchy from crying, the gash on her upper arm angry and congealed. Again, Peta longs to reach out in comfort, but now it is her feeling of having let Vira down that holds her back, along with her awareness that touch would not be welcome to a body that's been violated. She can only hope that her proximity and material help will communicate her deep concern and regret.

VIRA

IT'S A LONG NIGHT. Vira catches the whiff of antiseptic when Peta starts to clean and dress her wounds with stinging efficiency. She feels the liquid dribbling down her scalp as Peta dabs at the matted blood in her hair with a cotton ball.

"I don't think you'll need stitches," says Peta when she tapes gauze over the gash on Vira's arm, "but we'll need to keep an eye on these."

Peta urges on Vira a slice of bread with hummus and a glass of warmed oat milk. She tries to get some of it down, but she has no appetite.

When the two police officers arrive, they take a protracted statement as Vira rakes through her memory, fumbling for the English words, trying to piece things together in order.

"Where did the alleged attack take place?" asks the hefty Black officer with the creaking shoes, the one who appears to be in charge.

"Bank Street. He pulled me in small street."

"Well, which was it?" There's an edge of impatience in the voice. "On Bank Street, or the small street?"

"He attacked me on Bank Street, and he pulled me to small street to try to … to …" she can't bring herself to say the word.

"He tried to assault her sexually," says Peta, "but she managed to get away."

The officer writes this down.

"What's the name of the side street?"

"I am sorry, I do not know the name," says Vira.

"Well, what number on Bank Street?"

"I do not know this."

The officer exchanges a look with his colleague, and Vira feels a prick of unease that they think she is making this up.

Peta jumps in. "She was almost home, so it was probably Madeira Street or Collington Avenue," she says.

The officer makes a note.

"I need to see some ID," he says.

Eye Dee? What is this? Vira looks at Peta for guidance.

Peta says, "Her passport was in her backpack when it was stolen."

The officer puts down his pen and studies Vira for a long moment.

"No ID?" he asks.

"Everything was stolen." Vira's imagination jumps forward to a scenario where she is deported because she has no formal identification, and she has nowhere to go…

"There are copies at the International Rescue Committee," Peta intercedes again, "and we will go and fetch them tomorrow. Meanwhile, I can vouch for her. I am her sponsor through the Uniting for Ukraine program."

The officer taps the end of his pen on the page. "We'll have to see those papers," he says.

"Yes, I understand," says Vira, hoping she can appease him with her acquiescence.

And it goes on in this way—like catch and release, with her emotions ratcheting up and down correspondingly—for over an hour. At long last the report is done, Vira signs it, and the police depart, taking their skepticism with them.

Peta studies her. "You poor thing. You look completely washed out. Come and take a soak in my tub; it will be more relaxing than a shower."

The idea is so heavenly that Vira feels her mouth stretching into a smile. Peta leads Vira to the bathroom and leaves her there with a plump towel, bath salts, and a scented candle.

Vira sits in the fragrant water, studying her scuffed feet, the raw skin on her grazed knees, the dark smudges of bruising that are starting to show on her shoulders where the backpack was wrenched off. Gently easing off the gauze on her arm, she studies the vicious-looking gash. She forces her mind to be blank and focuses on the warm water against her skin, the fragrant steam around her. She soaks and scrubs, trying to scour away all traces of her ordeal.

When she climbs out of the bath, she looks at herself in the foggy mirror. She wipes the surface with the palm of her hand and stares into her eyes as she combs through the tangle of her wet hair, gingerly passing over the wound at the crown of her head. She pulls her hair back, the loose, dark strands falling over her forehead. Half closing her eyes, she sees Sevastyan staring back at her out of green, heavily lidded eyes. She wants more than anything in the world to be able to call him, to have him steady her with his reason and logic.

"Sevastyan," she murmurs at her reflection.

As identical as she and Sevastyan are in feature, they are different in personality. He is confident and outgoing, with his extraordinary gift for mathematics and computers. She is introverted and shy, and her language is music. She feels socially naked without him to be her face to the world. She wishes, not for the first time, that she could *be* like him, and not just look like him; that instead of feeling so exposed and diffident she could inhabit his confident body, albeit a damaged one. Missing him and fretting about him living every day in danger have become a constant counterpoint to everything she does—like a ground bass in music. Now, that is overlaid with bleak hopelessness about losing her phone and her essential lifeline to him. She keeps worrying away at his Telegram message: *Military medical commission says unfit to serve in military!* What had he meant by that? How will she ever find out now?

It is midnight before she finally climbs into bed. She is afraid to close her eyes, fearful that she will keep reliving the incident over and over in her mind. But she falls asleep almost immediately, and only wakes when the soft, persistent knocking on her door gets louder.

"Vira?" Peta calls through the door.

"Yes?" Vira's response is muffled and groggy in her ears.

"I'm sorry to wake you, but it's nine o'clock. I think the sooner you can see your person at the IRC the better."

"Yes. Thank you. I will come now."

Peta has brewed coffee, poured orange juice, and laid out fruit and granola. Next to the place that Peta has set for Vira is an iPhone.

Peta says, "This was my wife's phone. I've charged it and removed all the personal information. If you get any calls or messages that were meant for her, you can just ignore or delete them."

Vira stares at the phone, nonplussed by the thoughtful gesture.

"I cannot pay for this," she says.

"No, no!" Peta jumps in. "It's just been sitting in a drawer. I'm glad if it can be of use."

Tentatively Vira picks up the phone. "You are kind," she says. "Thank you."

As Vira eats her breakfast, Peta reads aloud from the news headlines on her phone; the Russian bombardment in the Donbas, the numbers of refugees, how many are being taken in by which countries. In between mouthfuls, Vira tells Peta about Sevastyan's ambiguous Telegram text.

"Do you think Sevastyan meant that *he* is unfit for military service?" Peta asks.

"It is possible. When he was teenager, he was with our mother when she was killed in traffic accident." Peta makes an inarticulate sound of dismay. "My brother had many operations for his back, where it was broken," Vira goes on, "and he has now—" What would the term be in English?

"Steel plates? Fused vertebrae?" guesses Peta.

"Something like this."

As Peta starts to clear the table and stack the dishwasher she says, "If he's not fit for military service, do you think he would be allowed to leave Ukraine?"

"I do not know this. There is still ... I think they call it martial law. President Zelenskyy said on television that all men from eighteen to sixty years old who are able may not leave country."

"So, I guess it depends on the definition of able," says Peta.

When Vira is ready to leave, Peta picks up her keys and slips her crossbody bag over her head.

"You are going out also?" Vira asks.

"I'm taking you."

"Oh, no—"

"Of course! I feel terrible that I wasn't with you yesterday."

Vira looks at Peta for a long moment. She is tall—almost six foot—and wiry. Her gray hair is cropped and spiky, and her blue eyes are set into a sharply angular face that belies her deep reserves of compassion. "Please, do not think this," Vira says. "It can happen in Lviv, or anywhere."

"But it happened while you are in my care," Peta says.

PETA

AT THE INTERNATIONAL RESCUE COMMITTEE, Fariba Mehta hands over duplicates of the copies of Vira's precious documents, and she enfolds her in a fragrant embrace with an easy spontaneity that Peta finds enviable. She also passes on the good news that the housekeeping job at Peabody has come through, and Vira can start tomorrow.

When Peta heads the Prius towards the 183 highway again for the southbound journey back she says, "I must just quickly stop at the grocery store on the way home."

Vira sits beside her, holding the folder of documents on her lap with her hands resting protectively on them. "I wish to prepare a meal for you," she says. "Please, may we buy some things?"

"You don't have to cook for me."

"But, please, I wish to. I will make for you Ukrainian meal."

Peta is reluctant to quash Vira's thoughtful gesture, but she feels she has to tell her that she's never been able to find much to eat at the Ukrainian festival because of being vegan.

"This is no problem. I will make vegan голубці with деруни."

Peta laughs. "I can't even imagine what those are," she says.

"Голубці is cabbage rolls with ..." she searches for the term, "something like rice ..."

"Grains?" offers Peta.

"Yes, grains," says Vira. "Sometimes, we call this 'little pigeons' because it looks little bit like. Деруни is potato pancake."

"Well, that all sounds mouthwatering," Peta says.

After a while Vira says, as if she has been pondering about this, "You are vegan, and you drive Prius, and you said Charm City Circulator is eco-friendly, and so I think you are ... one who cares about health of the world?"

"An environmentalist; yes, I am," says Peta. "In my work, I study the human impact on marine life and ecosystems, so even if I hadn't been an environmentalist before, I would have become one after seeing the way that human activity has affected ocean warming, and food beds, and things like that."

"What is your work?"

"I'm a marine biologist. Specifically, my department works on trying to restore the health of the Chesapeake estuary."

"What is this, please?"

Peta glances over at her. What must it be like, trying to live in a language that is not your own?

"An estuary is a body of water where a river meets the sea," says Peta. She scrolls, a little desperately, though her mind to try to think of a point of reference for Vira. "I believe there are estuaries that empty into the Black Sea."

"Ah yes, near Odesa in south of Ukraine, I think," says Vira. "But your one is not in good health?"

"No. The Chesapeake Bay is the biggest estuary in the United States," says Peta, "with more than a hundred and fifty major rivers and streams flowing into it from six surrounding states as well as Washington, D.C. And the problem is that not all our neighbors are careful about the effluent—the waste—they allow to flow through, so it lands up in the bay, and upsets the delicate balance of marine life."

Peta spots a rare parking place on the street near Whole Foods Market in Harbor East, and adroitly reverses the Prius into the space.

They don their face masks and, inside the store, Peta watches Vira's eyes travel over the open, semi-industrial area, with its abundant produce. She wonders what grocery stores were like in Ukraine, even before the invasion and the destruction and the shortages.

"Is this very different from a grocery store in Ukraine?" she asks.

"Not very different," says Vira. "This is little bit like Silpo supermarket in Lviv."

While Peta selects a bunch of organic bananas, Vira picks up a white cabbage, balancing it in her hands with a focused absorption. Peta wonders at her resilience; at her ability to take pleasure in something as mundane as a cabbage after the trauma of last night, and the upheaval of leaving Ukraine. *I should try to learn from her,* she thinks. Vira places the cabbage into the shopping basket, then adds five medium-sized potatoes, two purple onions, and a bunch of bright carrots. They wander the aisles until Vira finds bulgur wheat and a can of chopped tomatoes. In front of the dairy produce, she stands undecided.

"What do you like for cream?" she asks Peta.

Peta reaches for the coconut cream, and adds it to the basket, along with vegan butter and almond milk.

When Peta uses her Apple Pay app to buy the groceries, Vira says, "When I am working, I will pay you back."

"Don't be ridiculous!" says Peta, touched and taken aback in equal measure. "After all you have been through, how can you even think of such a thing?"

Vira gives a little self-deprecating shrug. "I must not be problem or worry for you."

Peta holds still to look at her, speaking seriously, "Vira, you're nothing of the kind."

Above her face-mask, Vira's green eyes glisten.

When they get back to the house, Vira unpacks the produce at one end of the long table in the kitchen, while Peta ensconces herself at the other end with her laptop.

"I'm not even going to offer to help!" she says.

"This is good," says Vira, "because I will say *no thank you*."

Peta has barely opened her laptop when the doorbell rings. She finds last night's police officers on the doorstep.

"Is Vira Blyzinskyj here?" asks the lead officer, making a good attempt at the pronunciation of her name.

"Vira!" Peta calls over her shoulder.

"We found your passport, ma'am," says the officer, handing it to Vira, his manner noticeably different now that he has tangible proof of her existence as well as the attack.

"And the phone?" In the hopeful eagerness of Vira's voice is all her yearning for that vital link back to her brother and her home.

"No, ma'am, no phone," he says. "But it looks like these documents are yours too." He proffers a bedraggled collection of papers. "It was all in a dumpster over by the Royal Farms convenience store on Fleet Street."

Vira takes the grubby documents from him. They will forever

carry the marks of her ordeal. "Thank you," she says.

"You're welcome, ma'am. And we'll keep the investigation open to search for the perpetrator." He takes a step backwards on his creaky shoes. "You have a good day, now," he says as he and his silent fellow officer turn to leave.

Peta closes the door and watches the jumble of emotions on Vira's expressive face.

"My phone," Vira says, bleakly.

"I know."

Vira takes a deep breath, then sets her mouth and turns to walk back into the kitchen. She places the soiled papers on the seat of a chair and flips to the back of her recovered passport. She pulls out a photograph and hands it to Peta.

Peta examines it. "When did you have short hair?" she asks.

"This is my brother," says Vira.

"My God!" Peta tilts the photograph towards the light of the window and studies it more closely. "You look identical," she says.

"When we were little, only our mother and father knew who we were."

"Was this taken recently?"

"Maybe six months."

"It's uncanny."

"What is this, please?"

"Strange. A little bit weird," says Peta looking at the photograph once more before handing it back.

"Uncanny," repeats Vira, as if tucking it away in her mind as she tucks the photograph into the back of her passport again.

Peta resumes her place at the table with her laptop and Vira carries the produce over to the sink to rinse it along with her hands. Over the running water, she says, "I have been thinking to cut my hair."

"Oh no!" It's an instinctive response before Peta can check herself. "It would be a shame to cut your beautiful hair," she adds.

"But I am thinking to look like my brother, to pretend to be him, so that I can feel more safe."

The idea is so far-fetched that Peta can't think of an appropriate response. Vira glances over her shoulder, evidently sensing her reservation.

"It's a terrible thing to happen to anyone, anywhere," Peta is carefully choosing her words, "but for you in a strange country, it's especially horrific."

She pauses, uncertain how to continue, and Vira goes back to scrubbing the carrots and potatoes.

Peta tries again. "I'm just not sure that pretending to be your brother is the best way to make you feel safe." Her scientific brain searches for a more feasible solution. "I can suggest a counselor you might like to see. She could help you process what happened."

Vira transfers the washed produce to a wooden board to start peeling and chopping. "Thank you," she says. "Maybe I will do this. But I am thinking maybe I was attacked because I am alone and a woman. If I am working at Peabody, I will be walking often on my own and riding on busses. If I can look more like a man, if I can look like my brother ..." she trails off, looking up and meeting Peta's eyes with an unspoken appeal for understanding.

Peta tries to respond to the entreaty by shifting her thinking to accommodate the notion of Vira impersonating her brother. "Well, you do look just like him," she says, "and it's true that gender distinctions are fluid these days..."

"These boots make me walk not so much like a woman." With the chopping knife in her hand, she crosses her arms over her chest with a self-effacing smile curling the corner of her mouth. "And I don't have so much here."

Peta smiles back. She had noticed. Still, her V-neck T-shirt falls over her body in a distinctly feminine way. "I guess it's possible that passing as a male could make you *feel* safer, and that might be half the battle," she says. "If you felt more confident, you'd probably come across as more confident and—one would hope—less vulnerable to attack."

Vira opens and closes a number of kitchen cabinets before she finds a couple of cooking pots. She fills the larger one with water, and lights the gas burner underneath it. In the other, she heats a cup of water and adds the bulgur wheat. Her activity is quick and economical, like a scientist working in a laboratory. A long strand of hair falls over her shoulder and Vira shrugs it away.

"What would you do about your hair?" asks Peta.

"I always cut my brother's hair. I hope it will not be so very difficult for me to cut my own hair in mirror."

Peta is far from sure about this. But she stops herself from saying anything more to douse the idea that Vira seems to have grabbed on to like a lifeline. It might conceivably stand a chance of helping her transition to her bewildering—and frightening—new environment.

Vira turns on the oven to preheat it, and, while the water in the big pot is coming to the boil, she cuts the stem from the cabbage before blanching the head in the boiling water and setting it aside to cool. Giving up any pretense of working on her grant, Peta watches as Vira starts to open and close cupboards again, looking for a saucepan. She pours oil into the pan to sauté the chopped onions and carrots, adds the cooked bulgur wheat, the canned tomatoes, and seasoning, then sets it all to simmer as she carefully starts peeling away leaves from the blanched cabbage. Every movement is graceful, her slender fingers deft.

"My wife was a jeans and T-shirt type of person," says Peta.

"She was bigger than you, but around the same height, so you can take a look and see if there's anything you could use."

Vira stops what she is doing and looks down the length of the table at Peta. "Thank you," she says.

"Let's see if we can make this work."

After a beat, another search ensues, this time for a casserole dish, which Vira layers with a couple of cabbage leaves. With a tablespoon, she measures out portions of the grain and vegetable mixture into the centers of the blanched cabbage leaves, rolling each one up and carefully placing it, seam down, in the casserole. She pours the remaining source over the *holubtsi,* and puts it into the oven.

"How long before we eat?" Peta asks. "It looks so delicious, I'm not sure I can wait."

Vira smiles. "It must cook an hour, or maybe more," she says. "But I will make now potato pancakes, and we can eat this while we wait."

ORSON

ORSON RUNS HIS HANDS OVER THE KEYBOARD in a series of
D-flat major scales—his favorite key, and the one he finds himself gravitating towards in this opera. This piano in his room at
Peabody isn't as good as his four-pedal Fazioli grand at home, but
he's hoping that the change of scene will help to focus his mind.
He fingers the elusive melody he's been struggling with, and mod-
ulates to the relative b-flat minor, feeling it out. And, this time, the
cadence works. He pulls some loose manuscript paper from the pile
on top of the piano, and his hand moves quickly across the page in
the dots and dashes of notation, breaking off now and then to finger something on the keyboard, as ideas begin to take form. He's
never taken to the music composition software programs that his
colleagues extol. For him there's something visceral, even sensual,
about the tactile contact with the page, as he tries to transform the
hovering musical patterns in his mind into a tangible form. He is

so engrossed as the tenuous melody line finally begins to take hold that time telescopes down to nothing.

The small clunk of the wastepaper bin being put down on the floor startles him as if it were a cymbal crash. He spins around on the piano bench, and that one movement is the tipping point for the piles of books and manuscript papers on the top of the piano. They slither in a slow-motion cascade onto the floor, and the more Orson tries to catch at them, the more the avalanche speeds up.

In the lull after the storm, Orson registers the person who put down the wastepaper bin and asks sharply, "Who are you?"

"I am from housekeeping. Sorry, your door was open."

Orson sizes up the intruder. They are wearing a face-mask over which a pair of startled and startling green eyes peer at him, and they have the androgynous look that a number of the students seem to be adopting these days.

"What's your name?"

After a fraction of hesitation, "Sevastyan."

So, the marker on the androgyny scale points slightly more to male, then, Orson decides.

"You gave me a shock," he says.

"I am sorry." Sevastyan kneels to pick up the nearest page, the angular forelock of his short cropped black hair falling across his forehead. He looks at the page intently for a moment, his head bowed, with more than cursory interest. As he begins to collect and stack the pages, Orson sees that he is arranging them in order, shuffling them around so that they follow sequentially.

"You read music," Orson observes.

"Yes."

Orson is not sure why this surprises him except that none of the other cleaners at the conservatory do, as far as he knows, and a number of his acquaintances regard it as an arcane skill, like reading hieroglyphics or code.

"Are you a musician?" Orson asks.

"I am music student."

"Here?"

"I am hoping."

"What's your instrument?"

"Viola da gamba."

Orson gives a short laugh of pure surprise. It's unusual enough for a cleaner to read music, but it's extraordinary that he would also play a rarefied Renaissance instrument. As Sevastyan reaches for the last scattered pages, his bony wrist extends from the cuff of his cotton shirt, and Orson registers that his hands look too slender and smooth for the rough work of cleaning.

"Are you hoping to get into the Historical Performance Department here?" Orson asks.

"Yes." Sevastyan stands up, holding out the neatly stacked manuscript pages. He is slight and young—barely out of his teens, by the look of it. "Where must I put these?" he asks. His voice has a light, tenor quality to it, and it's shaded by an unusual accent.

Orson reaches for the stack of pages and takes them wordlessly.

"May I dust the piano?" Sevastyan asks.

Orson waves the stack of papers towards it. "Go ahead!" he says.

He knows that he should try to keep working while the ideas are coming, but something holds him still. He is intrigued, and a little mystified. Sevastyan takes a cloth from his cleaning bucket, and starts systematically moving the clutter off the piano to wipe it down.

"Why did you choose viola da gamba?" Orson asks.

"I studied first cello, and I can play also Ukrainian folk instrument, *basiola*. This is little bit like viola da gamba."

"You're Ukrainian?"

"Yes."

"My God! You've been going through a rough time over there."

"Yes," says Sevastyan in such a low voice that Orson only just catches it.

Orson watches this quiet, self-contained young man as he keeps dusting, and he tries to envision what Sevastyan must have come from. Orson himself has lived through three major moves—from Pittsburgh to Juilliard in New York, and then here to the Peabody in Baltimore—and each one has been discombobulating in its unique way. He can't even begin to think what it must be like to have to leave a country, probably as a refugee, to travel halfway across the world.

"Well," Orson says, "let me know if there's any way I can help."

Sevastyan's green eyes flash up, then, to meet Orson's briefly, before he goes back to his work. As Orson continues to watch him—seeing but not seeing, half wanting to get back to his own work, half held here by this unusual person—his mind starts to feel its way around a germinating idea.

"What's the construct of a typical viol ensemble?" he asks.

Sevastyan stops his work and looks over at Orson, his eyes catching the light in the room. Orson registers him properly for the first time, noticing with surprise how striking he is, even with half his face obscured by a mask.

"In a consort, it is usual to have sets of viols in three sizes—treble, tenor, bass," Sevastyan says. "We call these chests."

"How many in each chest?"

"Between two and six."

"Can it be bigger?"

The green eyes crinkle into what Orson assumes is a smile. "It can be anything you want," Sevastyan says.

Orson thinks about this for a moment, and Sevastyan turns to stack the last manuscripts on the piano. In the quiet of the room, there is just the slight crackle and thump of papers as the piles of music are ordered. Dust motes, disturbed by the activity, hang in a slant of sunlight. Sevastyan drops the cloth into the cleaning bucket, picks it up, and starts heading for the door.

"I'm writing an opera," says Orson quickly to detain him, and Sevastyan stops, half turning. "It's set in the Renaissance." Orson hesitates, feeling his way, thinking aloud. "I'm wondering . . ." He trails off. "I've been trying to write something that is new and different, but that still suggests the period. I'm wondering if it would be possible to use a consort of viols as the orchestra."

Sevastyan stands considering him, the cleaning bucket still in his hand. "Your music, it is . . ." he searches for the word, "current . . . modern?"

"Yes, but it's tonal, so you see that's what would make it interesting—contemporary music played on instruments from the Renaissance."

Sevastyan nods, thoughtful, as if trying to conjure the music in his head.

"But I've never composed for period instruments before," Orson goes on, "much less a chest of viols." He studies this singular individual standing near the door with a cleaning bucket. Sevastyan could be an invaluable resource if Orson pursues this nascent idea. Of course, he could always consult with the historical performance department here at Peabody, he thinks, but this might be a way to help Sevastyan adapt to his radically different environment, while at the same time also being of incalculable benefit to Orson himself. "Would you be able to give me some pointers? I'd pay you, of course."

Sevastyan regards Orson steadily, his face shuttered, as if weighing options. Then he says, "I can try."

VIRA

THE NEXT DAY, Vira stands for a moment outside the door of orson's room at the music school to collect herself. She studies the nameplate: Dr. Orson Carradine. When she left yesterday, she'd looked for the name outside his room out of simple curiosity, and then spent quite a few moments trying to get her head around the fact that the person on the other side of the door was the same one who had composed the music for *The Hottentot Venus*. That CD had been ardently passed around from student to student at the Lviv Conservatory when it was released, and even though Vira's passion was already focused on the early music period, she'd been intrigued by the work's unique inventiveness and, at times, gorgeous lyricism. This person who had asked for her help seemed too unassuming, too gauche even, and too young to be someone who could have composed music like that.

Vira tries to calm her jumpy excitement by thinking herself

into the steady, pragmatic persona of Sevastyan. She raises her hand, and knocks.

"Come in!"

He is seated at the piano when she enters.

"Hi again," he says. He stands quickly, unfolding his body to its six-foot-plus height. "Hey! Is that your viol?"

"Yes."

"Great! I can't wait to see it, but I'll tell you a little bit about the project first. Just prop it in the corner for now."

He moves a pile of books from one of the upright chairs so she can sit down, and seats himself on the piano bench again, pushing it out a bit so that he can turn to face her. Then he seems to run out of steam. He drags his fingers through his dark hair, but it does nothing to tame the coiled tendrils. His wiry frame is hunched forward as he holds his hands between his knees, bouncing one of his legs up and down. He is more on edge than he was yesterday—nervous almost.

"Well," he begins, "here's a bit of background. Are you familiar with Shakespeare's play, *Twelfth Night*?"

"Yes."

"And have you heard of the Twelfth Night Festival in New England?"

"No."

"Well, it's a small festival outside of Boston that presents new, sometimes avant-garde works, and I've been commissioned to write a one-act opera for them next January," he says. "So, my director and I came up with the idea of building it around the comic characters in Shakespeare's play."

"Like Malvolio?"

"Exactly." He smiles, and it transforms his face. He goes on. "There's a precedent for using Shakespeare's work as a jumping off point to make something new, because Shakespeare himself based

Twelfth Night on a number of different sources."

This is fascinating. Shakespeare has always stood in Vira's mind as a singularly innovative genius, like Bach or Leonardo.

"The earliest source," Orson goes on, "was a comedy from 1531 called—I'm probably going to screw up the pronunciation—*Gl'ingannati*. Do you speak Italian?"

"No."

"I don't either, but apparently it means 'The Deceived Ones.' There were subsequent versions that Shakespeare used too, but they all essentially revolved around similar themes of mistaken identity, and the wrong people falling in love with each other, and a woman dressing up as a man, and so on."

At the mention of a woman dressing up as a man, Vira feels a little flip of her heart. She concentrates on keeping her face neutral.

"But the *subplot*," says Orson, fortunately oblivious to her little jab of discomfort, "with the business about Malvolio and the letter and the yellow stockings and that stuff, that was all Shakespeare's own invention—and that's what we've based our comic opera on."

"Does it have only those characters from ..." she searches her mind for the word he used, "subplot?"

"For the most part, yes, but Olivia's also in it," he says. "It's a chamber opera, so there are just six singers. Olivia is a coloratura soprano. Malvolio is a baritone; Maria's a mezzo soprano; Sir Toby Belch a bass; Andrew Aguecheek a countertenor; and Feste the Fool is a tenor."

"This is good. It is the range for the viol family."

"Which would be . . .?"

She weighs how best to describe it. It would be difficult even if she were speaking in her native tongue. "Let us use violin family to compare," she says. "But, to be clear, violas da gamba do not belong to this family."

"Oh? I've always thought the cello evolved from the viola da gamba."

"Many people think this because they look almost similar. But viols have more strings, and also frets like guitars, so I think my viola da gamba is cello's cousin, not her sister."

Orson nods and smiles in recognition at her analogy.

She pauses to collect her thoughts. "Yesterday, I told you that in viol consorts we have usually treble, tenor, and bass."

"Right, I remember, in a chest."

"Yes, and this is close to violin, viola, and cello. But we have, actually, seven sizes of viol. *Pardessus de viole* is smallest with highest pitch. Then comes treble, alto, tenor, bass, and two sizes for contrabass."

Orson is watching her intently, his pupils so large that his brown eyes look black. "Okay, so if I wanted to write a leitmotif for each character on the instrument that matched their voice, would the treble viol be for Olivia?"

"Yes."

"Come and take a look at the score and help me to work this out!" he says.

Vira stands and reads over his shoulder from the score on the piano's music rack.

"The tenor viol will be for Feste the clown," she says, "and bass viol for Malvolio."

"Okay, so that's your basic treble, tenor, and bass."

"For others, Maria's voice matches with alto viol, and it will be funny, maybe, if you use *pardessus de viole* for countertenor."

Orson laughs. "Sir Andrew, yes that works."

"And contrabass for Sir Toby," she says.

She sees his thoughts turn inwards as he hears the music in his head. Then he focuses on her again. "Which do you play?" he asks.

"Bass viol, which is close to equal with cello."

"So that would be Malvolio's voice," he says.

"Yes. But like with orchestra, different viols can accompany different voices also," she says. "And, just to say, viol sound—it is softer, more gentle, than violin family, so it is important you compose with care to balance with voices."

She sees his inner ear at work again. Then he says, "If I were to play the soprano line of Olivia's aria on the piano, could you play the instrumental line, so that I can hear how it sounds on viola da gamba?"

"I can try."

She stands and starts to unpack the viol and bow. She is suddenly jumpy with nerves and she fumbles with the openings on the instrument case. She has sight-read music countless times before, but there seems to be more at stake now, as if both she and her instrument are on trial. She's never played for someone this well known before, and she doesn't want to fall short of Orson's evident expectations.

The only score is the one on the piano rack, so she pulls the upright chair close enough to read and sits again, supporting the viol between her knees and calves. The familiarity of the movements, feeling her body respond to the contours of her instrument, helps to calm her tension a little.

"Do you tune to an A?" Orson asks.

"That will be fine," she says.

Orson plays the note for her and, when she looks up from tuning, he is watching her closely. She feels a flush run over her skin. This is the closest they have ever been to each other physically, and she is aware now of Orson's faint scent—a mixture of cotton and butter.

"Just so you know, this comes from the second scene of the opera," he says. "In the first scene, we've already met Olivia's uncle,

Sir Toby Belch, who's brought Sir Andrew Aguecheek to Olivia's house to woo her. In the second scene, there's some banter between Olivia's lady-in-waiting, Maria, and Feste the Fool, and we meet Malvolio for the first time. Then comes Olivia's aria, and it's all about loss and mourning." He glances at her. "Okay?"

"Yes, I understand."

In her head, Vira sight reads the opening phrase, and then plays it on the viol. Just after the modulation, Orson comes in with Olivia's vocal line. The way the musical phrases touch, then blend and interweave is almost discordant, but not quite—they flirt, they dart away, and they resolve so poignantly that Vira feels as if she has to hold her breath to play it. When they finish, they sit unmoving, the last chord fading, their eyes still on the music. The music is so new, so inventive, so unlike anything Vira has ever heard or played. And this man sitting next to her made it. What is at the core of a person who can make something so exquisite? What kind of man is this Orson Carradine if he can create something that makes her feel like this? She blinks away unshed tears.

"It is beautiful," she says. "Very beautiful."

"It sounds better than I dared to hope on the viol."

"Do you know yet who will sing it?"

Orson wipes his hand across his face. "*Ah, there's the rub*, as Hamlet would say. I wrote it specifically for Isabella Foiani's voice, but she says she's withdrawing from all public performances."

"Oh, she is perfect for this!"

"You know her?"

"Only from *The Hottentot Venus*," she says.

Orson stares at her, and she feels the dynamic between them shift.

He says, "I didn't know you were familiar with that."

She wonders if she has given too much away. Her goal is to be unobtrusive, unremarkable, low key, so that she can hide behind being something she isn't. Walking to and from the Charm City Circulator these past days, assuming the persona of Sevastyan has given her a curious sense of inconspicuous invulnerability, and she's welcomed that feeling.

Orson continues to look at her intently, but she can tell that his thoughts have turned inward again, and he is not really seeing her.

Suddenly he says, "Maybe *you* could be the one to persuade Isabella to do it."

Vira gives a short laugh at the absurdity of the idea.

"No, I'm serious," says Orson. "Why not? I've tried, over and over, and now she won't even talk to me about it. My director has tried—but she's stopped communicating with him, too. I'm desperate." He runs his hands through his tangle of hair again. "It *has* to be her. I'll try anything to break through to her. Perhaps that could be you. Just pitch up! Don't give her any time to put up any barriers. Why not?"

"Excuse me, but this is stupid idea," Vira says. "She will never listen to refugee student from Ukraine."

"But she might. I'm fascinated by your story and your musical knowledge, and I think she would be, too," Orson says. "It's worth a try. I've tried every approach I can think of, but it's complicated with me because ... well, she knows I still hold a torch for her."

"Torch?"

"I've had a thing for her ever since we were at Juilliard together."

Vira stands so that she can make a business of putting the viol away in its case, to give herself something practical to do while she tries to sort through her jumbled thoughts. She feels a hollow pang at the thought of Orson having feelings for Isabella Foiani. But of *course*, he would! She's exquisite, to judge by her photographs, and they are in the same league musically. Vira packs away her instrument with efficient familiarity, while she feels herself to be the exact opposite—like a handful of intractable springs that she is trying to cram into a too-small box. She knows that he is watching her, and it makes her all the more self-conscious as she tries to formulate a good exit line so she can go away to be by herself and think.

"Listen," Orson says, "you said yourself Isabella is perfect for this role. If she insists that she won't do it and we have to try to find someone else, it's not going to be the same. Just go and talk to her! She lives in a loft apartment in The Standard over on St. Paul's Street. It's within easy walking distance. You're my last resort."

Vira stands perfectly still with her hand resting on her viol case, as if keeping contact with her instrument will somehow ground her and give her confidence. She knows that she should say no. Her whole objective in taking on this pretense of being Sevastyan is to try to blend into the background.

But, in this room, alongside this strange, unpredictable, extraordinarily gifted man, she has just played some of the most sublime music she's ever heard. It's like in an improbable dream, being in the same room, playing the music of a composer whose work has intrigued her from afar. And now, he's presenting her with an opportunity to meet a singer whose voice she has admired just as much from afar. There's no doubt that she is star struck by them both. Within days of arriving in America, aside from being jumped, she's met a celebrated musician, and is being offered the opportunity of meeting another.

Against her better judgment, knowing that it stands every chance of putting her flimsy cover at risk, she finds she can't resist. If Orson Carradine thinks that by some wild off-chance she might be able to bring to his music the voice that would truly do it justice, she will go along with his far-fetched scheme.

"Okay," she says.

ISABELLA

THE BIALETTI COFFEE POT starts to bubble on the stovetop and Isabella turns off the gas flame. It's Malvon's day to be here and she needs the fortification of caffeine to get through his visit. He is superb at managing her business affairs, and she can't even begin to imagine the state they would be in by now without him, but his pedantic manner is wearing. She pours the coffee into a white Arzberg mug, taking pleasure, as always, from its clean, delicate design, and she wanders listlessly through to the music room, which doubles as an office.

Malvon is working at her antique pedestal desk, and he stands when she comes in, as he does every single time she enters a room. She would almost expect him to doff his hat, if he had one. His mouse brown hair is combed as usual into formidable neatness, and his pale blue eyes seem to swim behind the thick lenses of steel rimmed glasses. The bow tie he has chosen for today has a vivid Prussian blue geometric design against a startling yellow background.

"So," she says, her tone over bright, "how are things looking?"

"Well," he says, and even that one syllable is exquisitely modulated in his lugubrious baritone, "since you have withdrawn from performance for the foreseeable future, there is not much to do. However, the royalties from your compact disc of Florence Price songs have started to come in, and I have attended to those. There was another inquiry from the Metropolitan Opera..." he leaves the phrase hanging for a moment. "Are you still quite resolved about not appearing during the next season?"

Isabella feels washed over with tiredness—she has gone over this issue countless times before. "I am still quite resolved," she says.

"Your gift ..." he murmurs. "Such a waste."

"Malvon, please!" She can hear the sharpness in her own voice.

The intercom pings from the concierge at the downstairs desk, and it brings her back to herself. She takes a deep, steadying breath.

"We've discussed this. I'm simply exhausted. I can't take on that endless cycle of touring and rehearsing right now."

He looks at her with a tragic furrow between his eyebrows, his narrow lips folded as if it is taking all his forbearance to keep himself from speaking.

Mía comes into the room, bringing with her the nimble energy that she carries around with her like an aura. In the year or so that Mía has been working for her, Isabella has come to rely on her for much more than simply keeping the apartment in beautiful order and preparing enticing meals.

"Fausto called up," says Mía. "There's a young guy downstairs who says he won't go away until he can speak with you, Isabella."

"Oh, God!" says Isabella. "It's probably Curtis about Orson's damn opera again. Malvon, since you're here, please will you go and put him off?"

Malvon inclines his head without speaking, and he sets off to perform his errand.

Isabella flops down in a chair, taking care not to slop the coffee in the mug she is still cradling. "Oh, Mía, it's all just too much. Why did I ever get into this business? Why won't people just leave me alone?"

Mía walks around to the back of the chair and starts to massage Isabella's shoulders and neck. "Oh, I can think of millions of reasons," she says. You're beautiful, you have an exquisite voice, you're famous, you're a money spinner—"

"Oh, stop it!" Isabella laughs, dropping her head forward on her slender neck, and relaxing into the gentle pressure of Mía's hands. She doesn't feel at all beautiful today. She's just dragged on a pair of ripped jeans and a T-shirt, and her cloud of black hair is raked up into a disheveled ponytail.

But it's on the inside that she feels most unlovely. She wakes each morning with such an insidious blackness crowding in on her that she feels there's no point to anything—not even to getting up. If it weren't for Mía, she would probably just curl up on her bed all day. It's Mía's routine and joyous insouciance that gives Isabella's day some shape, and, come the evening, her life feels less bleak— only for the cycle to begin all over again the next day.

The front door clicks shut, signaling Malvon's return, and he slides into the room on his silent Hush Puppies. "The young man downstairs is intransigent about speaking with you, Miss Foiani," he says. He persists in addressing her formally even though she has repeatedly invited him to call her Isabella.

"Is it Curtis?" asks Isabella.

"No. He says his name is Sevastyan." Malvon puts extra emphasis on the last syllable of the name. "However, he *is* an ambassador for Dr. Carradine."

"Did you tell him that I am not at home?"

"I did, but he said that he would wait until you returned."

"Couldn't you just tell him that I am indisposed?"

"I said as much, and he replied that what he has to tell you will make you well."

This person seems more insistent, even, than Curtis.

"What's he like?"

"He's some..." he pauses to choose his word carefully, *"foreigner."*

The patent disdain in his voice makes Mía speak up, "There's nothing wrong with being a foreigner!" she snaps.

The fiery courage of Mía's convictions is one of the many endearing things about her, and Isabella can tell that Malvon has touched a nerve. When Isabella had returned home to Baltimore, deciding to make it her base after Juilliard and the first hectic years on the singing circuit, it was her brother who suggested that Mía might come and work for her. Julian had acted as the immigration lawyer for Mía's family during their long years of living in the shadows, guiding them through the precarious process of becoming permanent residents in the States. Having known Isabella all his life and having come to know Mía over the years, he'd had a feeling that they would get on. He was right.

Isabella turns to look at Malvon, trying to judge his response to Mía's sharp retort. He maintains a stiff reserve.

"I meant, what sort of person is he?" says Isabella into the awkward silence.

"He's young," says Malvon, keeping his eyes fixed on Isabella, and pointedly ignoring Mía. "In fact, his manner belies his years. Despite his recalcitrance, he seems well bred. He has a..." again, the hesitation, "foreign accent, but a fair grasp of the English language. I estimate that he is five foot ten or eleven in height." Malvon pauses, as if going over a mental checklist. "One can't help but notice his rather unusual eyes," he concludes.

"Oh?" queries Isabelle.

"They are emerald green," says Malvon.

Isabella draws air deep into her lungs in the way she has trained to do as a singer. "Oh, all right," she says. "Let's get this over with. I'll see him in the drawing room."

"I'll tell Fausto to send him up," says Mía. "Do you want me to stay with you?"

"No, it's okay. This shouldn't take long," says Isabella, handing over her now empty coffee mug.

She walks into the long living room. At the kitchen end is an oval walnut dining table with chairs. In the corner, near the high windows, a spiral staircase leads up to her bedroom. She turns on the classical music station. A Beethoven string quartet is playing, but she can't quite place which one. She chooses the chair with the ottoman, picks up *The New Yorker*, and pages to Music in *Goings on About Town*. She can't focus. Beethoven was Julian's favorite composer, and she can't hear any of his music without being reminded of him. Even now, six months after his death, she can only think of Julian in small snatches before she begins to feel adrift again in grief.

She closes her eyes, and rests her head back against the chair. Would she be less anguished if she didn't feel such self-reproach about not being with Julian at the end? She still can't get over the way she misjudged that so terribly. The cancer had dragged on for almost a year after his diagnosis, and when the physicians at the hospice told her that he was just there for monitoring, she was so sure that there would be time to sing that final performance of *La Traviata* at the Sarasota Opera Festival before she went to be with him, to take him back to his home and take care of him. But she had been too late by one day. One day. How can she ever forgive herself? How could one more opera performance be more important than seeing her brother one last time? How can she ever sing again in the face of that question?

She hears the knocker on the front door, and Mía's quick foot-steps across the hall in response.

"I am here to see Isabella Foiani." The visitor's voice has a light tenor timbre, and it is touched by a Slavic accent.

"Come this way," says Mía.

Isabella looks towards the open doorway, trying to take on a calm expression. The young man who appears is slim and lithe, though he is dressed in shapeless jeans and T-shirt. He wears a face-mask and it is as Malvon said—it's impossible not to be drawn to his eyes. The two assess each other in silence for a moment.

"Would you like to sit down?" asks Isabella.

"Thank you." He perches on the edge of the nearest chair as if he might spring up and bolt at any moment. He regards her with those extraordinary eyes.

"Well?"

"Excuse me, but you are Isabella Foiani?"

"Yes, I am she."

"You do not look like your photographs."

Isabella feels a little stung by this, as if it underscores her feel-ings of unloveliness. The Beethoven string quartet comes to an end, and the back-announcement identifies it as the first Razumovsky quartet. Ballet music by Tchaikovsky will be up next.

"Well," says Isabella again, "I think I can guess why you are here."

"Orson Carradine has composed beautiful music for you to sing."

"As I have told him repeatedly, I am not performing at the moment."

"But this is not like other performing. It is music that he made especially for your voice."

"Oh, come now! No voice is as unique as that. I am a soprano; I have a good ear for intonation; I have a competent sense of rhythm; I have mastered coloratura technique; I can sing in a range of styles. Any professional singer could lay claim to those qualities. None of them makes me unique."

"These things you list, they are what is outside. It is what is inside you that makes you... unique, as you say. It is how you understand music in your heart."

"Were you sent here to flatter me?"

"No. I know your voice from *The Venus Hottentot*, and I have heard Orson Carradine's music also in his new opera. No other soprano can sing it like you."

Isabella studies this unusual young man who speaks with such simple authority. For a moment—just a moment—his praise of the music and her voice is alluring, almost tempting.

"What is it?" she asks.

"It is someone who mourns her loss. It is music that is sad, but also in it there is longing... and hope." He pauses, his face alight. When she doesn't respond, he says, "It goes forward and back in modulations between major and minor. It is old and new all at once."

Isabella looks away from his animated face to the bright day outside. The brightness is like an insult to the leaden feeling inside herself. Why can't anyone understand that she is too tired—too depleted—to give herself over to the voracious needs of composers and directors and fellow musicians and audiences?

"I can't..." she begins, but suddenly she can't trust herself to speak further because she feels emotion tightening her throat.

In the silence between them, the Tchaikovsky excerpt comes to an end on the radio. The announcer introduces a Handel aria, and, after a short instrumental introduction, Isabella's own voice bursts into the room. It is velvety and true, with the purity of a boy's treble voice, but the warmth of a quickly vibrating violin.

Sevastyan abruptly stands and crosses the room to sit on the ottoman next to Isabella's feet. "Miss Foiani!" She turns her face to him, startled. "If I had your gift, as ... as wonderful as it is, I would never, ever hold it back. I could not do it."

"What would you do?"

"I would have to *share* it ... like when a drop in water makes waves to spread out in circles getting bigger and bigger. Like..." he seems to grope for the word, "like echoes that you hear over and over." His eyes dart intently from one to the other of hers. "I would do *everything* to keep it alive, and I ... I would protect it every moment of every day and night, like something I loved ... a child ... or a lover ... or a brother." He lowers his voice. "And, even if it was difficult, if it made me sad, I could not let it go. I would give my life to it."

Isabella looks into the green eyes that are fixed on her. "Your child or your lover or your brother would be blessed," she says. She reaches for the remote, and clicks off the radio mid note. She doesn't want her voice competing with this passionate young man. "How do you know Orson's music so well?"

"He played Olivia's aria—your aria—and I accompanied him on viola da gamba."

"Viola da gamba!"

"He thinks he will use viol consort as orchestra."

Against her will, Isabella's interest is piqued. "Viola da gamba," she says again. "Is that your specialization?"

"I am not ... specialist, but I play viola da gamba, yes."

She studies him. This Sevastyan is intriguing. He is young, to judge by his looks, but extraordinarily mature and accomplished for his age.

"How old are you?" Isabella asks.

He considers her. "I guess around your age."

"I doubt it," says Isabella.

She holds his eyes for a moment and then turns her head away to look out of the window again. A woman in mourning ... longing ... hope ... old and new. Curtis didn't describe the music this way. Neither did Orson himself. The simple urgency of this young man has touched something deep under the weight of her lethargy, and she feels it stir.

Mía's quick steps cross the entrance hall, and the music room door opens to the accompaniment of clucking complaints from Malvon. Isabella stands, and Sevastyan follows suit.

"I'm not committing to anything," she says, "but if you come again and bring your instrument with you, we can read through the aria."

MÍA

MÍA STEPS OFF THE ELEVATOR of Isabella's apartment building into the high vaulted lobby with its Tennessee pink marble and potted palms.

"Hi, Mía," says Fausto from his front desk facing the entrance, "On your way home?"

"Yes," says Mía.

"Will you be in tomorrow?"

"No, Isabella says she doesn't need me this weekend."

Fausto Giullare, plump and genial, has been the concierge since the Beaux Arts Standard Oil Building was turned into luxury apartments twenty years ago. There is nothing he doesn't know about the goings on, and Mía feels an affinity for him as a fellow immigrant.

"So, what did that obstinate young Sevastyan want with Miss Foiani?" Fausto asks.

"Oh, he's just someone else who wants her to go back to singing," she says, "but I think he made quite an impression on her in his way."

"A horse that won't move makes quite an impression, too!"

Mía laughs and waves goodnight as she walks through the ornate brass doors onto St. Paul's Street and into the tepid evening. It's about a ten-minute walk to the studio apartment she rents on North Calvert, and she uses the time to think through an *ajiaco* soup recipe she's been wanting to try out, substituting jackfruit for chicken. What yoga does for some, cooking does for Mía. She finds herself grounded by the combination of creativity and practicality, while the smells, textures, colors, tastes are like a sensual heaven that transports her back to her *abuelita*'s kitchen in Colombia. Her grandmother is a superbly inventive cook, and though her flair skipped a generation—Mía's mother can't even be bothered to toast a slice of bread—it blossomed again in Mía. When the family was finally able to visit Colombia again after they were legal residents, Mía found her métier in her *abuelita*'s steaming, fragrant kitchen.

Mía knows that one of these days or months or years, before she gets too far into her twenties, she'll probably go to college. But for now, she loves taking care of Isabella's beautiful apartment and occasionally tempting her with one of her culinary creations. She feels herself much more than just a housekeeper for Isabella. Having grown so attached to Julian while he was helping her family, she urgently wants to support Isabella in her aching sorrow about her brother's death. Mía has never lost anyone really close to her, but she knows about the longing of separation, with her parents in Miami and their extended family still in Colombia.

Her father had been alarmed when Mía followed a now-ex boyfriend to the treacherous north, and he'd harangued her until he'd been able to come and see for himself that she was living a safe and comfortable life. Her mother meanwhile, single-minded as ever, continues to work away in her biochemistry lab in Florida, more or less oblivious to the world around her.

Her mother is the reason that the family came to the United States in the first place. She'd attended a scientific conference in Miami in the late 1990s, during the time that the armed conflict and political violence in Colombia were escalating. Seeing an opportunity to stay in the U.S. through the contacts she made at the conference, she jumped at it. She brought Mía, just eighteen months old, and, after some years, her husband had managed to come too.

Even though there was some legitimacy to Mía's mother being in America through her scientific work, it was a traumatic time. On Julian's advice, the family had saved every single scrap of paper relating to their lives—medical records, school reports, tax returns—so that he would eventually be able to argue for their right to be legal residents. It was sixteen years before they could finally get their green cards and live without fear of being thrown out of the country at any minute.

Mía was so young when she came to America that it's the only country she really knows, but too often she feels like an outsider—not fully American but not Colombian either. It's why the comment about "some foreigner" from the insufferable Malvon had stung the way it did.

At home, Mía clicks on the Spanish language radio station and pours herself a glass of red wine. She heats olive oil in a large soup pot and browns a chopped onion and two minced garlic cloves. She adds four cups of vegetable stock, throws in a cup of chopped cilantro leaves, two sliced spring onions, and adds salt and pepper. She hasn't been able to find any of the *guascas* herb, so she substitutes oregano, even though it has a more bitter taste than the subtle, artichoke-like flavor of *guascas*.

While all of this is reducing, she calls her father in Miami. Her mother rarely comes to the phone, generally just calling out her contributions in the background. Relaxing into the easy flow of Spanish on the phone with her parents is like slipping into a warm bath at the end of the day.

"I sold a painting," her father tells her.

"Undersold it, more like," calls his wife.

Mía's father goes to the former warehouse district north of Miami most days while her mother's life is taken up with her esoteric research. He's had an artist's studio in the district since before the area became a trendy arts hub, and he goes there to paint richly colored canvases that evoke the Pre-Columbian period.

"Remember that time *papa* was selling a miniature," her mother calls, "and you decided to step in and talked the dealer into paying almost double?"

Mía laughs. "Tell her I'm still very proud of that."

Her father relays the message. "That was crazy," he says. "How old were you—fifteen?"

"Fourteen, I think."

As they chat back and forth, Mía stirs the soup mixture from time to time, and when they eventually hang up, she adds a pound of mixed potatoes—red, gold, russet—cut into bite-size pieces. Once those have cooked through, she tips the shredded jackfruit to the mix, and simmers it for another five minutes. She chooses not to add the traditional pieces of corn on the cob—they're not aesthetically pleasing to her—but when she dishes up her portion into a serving bowl, she tops it with white rice, sliced avocados, cream, and capers. She carries her helping through to the small, round table next to the kitchen area, and tucks in as she scrolls through her various social media platforms, "liking" the food posts.

Once she's had her fill—*ajiaco* being a whole meal in itself—she saves a portion to take to Isabella on Monday, and wipes down the kitchen efficiently enough to do a celebrity chef proud. Satisfied, she takes a lengthy, aromatic shower, and climbs into bed for an early night, pulling one of the cookbooks from the stack on her nightstand. It's the best way to wind down the day for her, browsing through recipes before she turns out the light.

She is jolted out of sleep by thunderous knocking on the front door of her apartment. She sits up so quickly that she gives herself a sharp crick in her neck, and the room swims around her. The thundering comes again, this time with shouts of "ICE—open up, please!"

Her heart is banging against her ribs. She's completely disorientated, but finds herself standing up, out of bed, dragging on a pair of sweatpants, and padding to the front door to peer through the peephole. She sees two uniformed men, their bulbous close-up faces shrinking to out-of-proportion bodies in the fish eye. She can hear other tenants in the apartment block querulously asking what is going on.

The beefy man nearest the peephole thunders on the door again.

Mía calls through the door, "Who is it?"

"Are you Mía García Moreno?" He pronounces her name "My-a" instead of "Mee-a."

"Yes."

"We need to see your papers."

It is what her family lived in fear of for sixteen years; that they would be found undocumented and be deported back to Colombia. Even now, she feels a jolt of panic. What if they find something wrong with her papers, and the ripple effect impacts her family? She knows full well that she is just a speck of dust against the steamroller of the immigration system, but she still remembers the rights that Julian drummed into all of them: *Don't open the door! Ask to see a warrant! Say you want your lawyer!* But she can no longer call on Julian.

"Do you have a warrant?" she calls through the door.

"Yes, we do."

How can this be happening? Why is this happening now, when her status is no longer in question?

"Push the warrant under the door!" she says.

First a corner of the document appears, and then the rest is shoved through. She turns on the light and looks for her name, her address, and a signature on the warrant. It is, indeed, a search warrant, signed by a judge, allowing the agents to search her home. It is quiet on the other side of the door. What can she do? If only it were possible to call Julian!

"Ma'am?" the voice comes through the door again. "The warrant gives us the right to search the premises."

"Please, I need a minute," she calls.

Mía turns away from the front door. She closes her eyes, trying to remember everything that Julian had instilled in them. *If they have a warrant, you're obliged to let them in. Ask to see identification. Say as little as possible.*

"Ma'am! You have to let us in."

"Just a minute, please."

Don't do anything that could make the situation escalate, Julian had said. *Show them your passport and, if they insist, your document of naturalization.*

Mía turns again to the front door.

"Please hold up your IDs so that I can see them."

The two agents do so, and she peers at their badges through

the peephole, trying to decipher them.

"Okay," she says. "Just wait while I fetch my papers."

She always carries her passport with her everywhere she goes, and she retrieves it now from the wallet in her purse. Just in case, she pulls down the box from a top shelf in her closet where she keeps her important papers, and takes out her document of naturalization. She squeezes her eyes shut, steeling herself, knowing that she can't put off the moment any longer. She walks to the door, unlocks it, and opens it.

The two agents step inside with their clumpy boots, the ICE insignia emblazoned on their uniforms. Mía feels crowded in and vulnerable. Silently, she proffers her United States passport. The beefy agent takes it, compares the photograph to her bed-tousled appearance, and shoots a look at his colleague, who shrugs.

"Okay, that will be all, ma'am, thank you," the agent says, handing her passport back. "Sorry for the inconvenience."

Almost before she realizes it, he has retrieved the search warrant, and they are gone. She listens to the tramp-tramp of their heavy boots as they walk away. Scattered lights from disturbed neighbors spill out onto the corridor.

Mía closes the door, locks it, and leans her back against it. She stands quite still, holding on to her precious documents, trying to make sense of what has just happened. These agents came to *her* door, demanding to see *her* papers. This wasn't part of some random roundup. She had been singled out. But why? And by whom? Do they have the right to go knocking on people's doors in the middle of the night on some wild fishing expedition? Surely a judge wouldn't sign off on something like that. Had the Immigration and Customs Enforcement received a tip-off about her in particular? She suddenly feels suspicious of everyone living in her apartment block, and mentally runs through the ones she's come across, speculating about who might be so mean-spirited. Who would do such a thing without grounds for suspicion? Even if someone *did* suspect that she was an illegal immigrant, she thinks, what would be in it for them to report it to ICE? Who would ever commit such an officious act of unkindness?

Malvon Steward.

His name pops unbidden into her mind, and it lodges there. *He* would have it in him to be that officious and unkind, she thinks. He is that annoying, and he evidently has a thing about foreigners. "Malvon," she thinks again.

SEVASTYAN

THE MOMENT THE AIRPLANE TOUCHES DOWN at Dulles International Airport and the flight attendant announces that cell phones may be used, Sevastyan checks for a message from Vira. Nothing. Even before Vira left Ukraine, they were always in constant contact with Telegram texts throughout the day. He's shared every detail of her trip to Poland, her months there as she tried to find a way to get to the United States, and, most recently, a flurry of Telegram messages about her flights, her safe arrival, and a meeting she'd set up at the International Rescue Committee. But, from one moment to the next, she went suddenly and inexplicably silent. He keeps re-reading the last message she sent while she was waiting to go in for her interview at the Rescue Committee, and there's been nothing since. He's texted constantly, but got no response. He's phoned, but his calls just go to voicemail. He knows she is being sponsored by someone from the Uniting for Ukraine program, but he doesn't know the person's name or how to contact them. He is frantic.

In the week after Vira left Ukraine, Sevastyan had gone to the territorial defense recruitment center on Pekarska Street in Lviv. He thought it would be a simple matter of signing up, but he was told he had to provide background information to verify that he was in good health and had no criminal record. Getting a criminal background check was straightforward, but he was brought up short by the health record. For almost ten years, he's lived with his spinal injury. Sometimes, the pain gnaws at him, and he walks with an almost imperceptible limp, but he's refused to allow it to dictate his life. Yet, according to the medical commission, it makes him unfit to serve in the military.

He'd been so single-minded in his determination to defend Ukraine that he was completely thrown of course by this obstruction. As he and Vira kept in touch about her process of seeking help from the Ukraine consulate in Krakow and finding a sponsor through the Uniting for Ukraine program, they had also been trying to think through ways that he could still support the cause at home, even if they wouldn't allow him to do military service. With Vira's abrupt silence, though, his commitment to serve began to swerve towards an urgency to try to get to the States to find out what on earth has happened to her. In the end, the medical exemption from the commission, instead of being a blight, has turned out to be a boon; it's one of the few extenuating circumstances for men of fighting age being allowed to leave the country.

Sevastyan has always been sanguine about finding solutions to convoluted problems, approaching them like mathematical calculations, both on and off the page. In record time, he secured a visa for the United States and a plane ticket out of Ukraine. But the invasion, the war, the chaos, the destruction—and the instability of anything being as it was, or ever being so again—have robbed him of his innate ebullience. He is desperate with worry about Vira, and exhausted from constantly trying to drag his imagination back from tipping into dire scenarios about why she has disappeared.

He presents his passport at the Dulles border control and the officer says, "Ukraine? Lots of you coming through here now." He asks Sevastyan to pull down his face-mask to compare his photograph with his face, and says, "What is the purpose of your visit?"

"I must find my sister. She came to America, but we lost contact." *Is this too much information? Is he talking too much?*

Apparently so, because the officer looks at him, weighing him up. "You will have to come with me, sir."

He steps out of his cubicle, and the two of them walk, unspeaking, through the stark airport to the nether regions. A uniformed officer in a back office is reading *The Washington Post*, and looks up reluctantly when Sevastyan is shown in.

Sevastyan is not invited to sit down, and the officer reaches his hand across his desk in an unspoken demand for his passport. The tourist visa in his passport, Sevastyan knows, is only to allow him into the country. It is meaningless without the stamp that will allow him to stay. That authority rests with this taciturn man.

"Ukraine," the officer says. "You're one of the lucky ones. Millions can't get out."

"I know this," says Sevastyan. "I am grateful."

"How come you're not fighting for your country, like all the other men your age?" The officer's evident disdain is like a noxious smell.

"I have spinal injuries, and medical commissioner says it makes me unfit to serve in military," he says, translating in his head what the commissioner told him in Lviv, and hoping the translation makes sense in English.

"You here as a refugee?"

"Not really. My sister came, but she disappeared. I am here to find her."

"Her name?"

Sevastyan tells him, spelling it out.

The officer types it in on his computer keyboard, and looks at the screen for the result. "Yes, Vira Blyzinskyj came in through BWI."

Sevastyan's stomach tightens at this proof that she is documented in the system, for good or ill.

"What's your occupation?"

"Quantum computing."

A flicker of interest then. "Oh yeah?" The officer looks at him for the first time.

"Yes. We apply quantum phenomena to problems with great numbers of variables and potential outcomes," says Sevastyan, more familiar with the English words for these arcane concepts than he is with more mundane ideas.

"Like how?"

Sevastyan tries to think of an example that will resonate with this officer. "We can, just for example, use qubits instead of usual computer bits to find, more quickly and powerfully, best routes of thousands of airplanes to fly around world."

"Wild!" says the officer. Then he becomes laconically all-business again. "You know you can't work in the United States on a tourist visa?"

"Yes."

"And you understand you can't overstay the six months on your visa?"

"I understand."

The officer flattens Sevastyan's passport on the desk, makes a stamp on it, and writes in a date. He hands the passport back and returns to his newspaper before Sevastyan has turned to leave.

Sevastyan takes a shuttle to an airport hotel and books a room for the night. He rides up in the elevator armed with pamphlets and maps from the lobby so that he can plan how to get to Baltimore tomorrow.

By the time he's settled into his room and bought a few items from the vending machine for a makeshift supper, it is 7:15 p.m., although according to his biological clock it's 2:15 the next morning. He sleeps in restless snatches—unusually for him—and he has a nagging, recurring dream of Vira at the far end of an aircraft cabin. Every time he takes a step towards her, she disappears through a different doorway in the overhead lockers.

When he wakes and finally pushes the dream away, his cell phone tells him it is five o' clock. His back has taken a beating from the long, cramped flights, and it throbs with the pulse of his heart. He eases carefully onto his side and snaps on the light, looking reflexively for a message from Vira. Nothing. It's too early to begin his real, on the ground search for her. He pushes himself upright sits on the edge of the unfamiliar bed, trying to think of her in this country, desperately hoping that she is somehow somewhere safe. Their lives have always been so inextricably shared that making any decision without the other's input is unthinkable. This severed communication is like losing one of his senses.

MÍA

MÍA OPENS THE DOOR TO THE MUSIC ROOM. Malvon glances up quickly from the desk. His look of expectancy shuts down when he sees Mía and not Isabella.

She'd anticipated that she would find him in the room, but still she finds his presence disconcerting. "Hi," she says.

"Good morning." He turns back to his work, tight-lipped.

Mía decides to test the waters. "I had a bad experience on Friday night," she says.

Malvon turns his eyes from his work again with marked reluctance, and they come to rest on a spot in her general direction.

"Immigration and Customs Enforcement came banging on my door at one o'clock in the morning with a warrant to see my papers."

Malvon's pale eyes flicker, but his face remains impassive. The silence lasts just a little too long, and then he says, "Well, they were simply doing their duty, no doubt."

"But it's weird they would single me out now, when I've been a U.S. citizen for two years."

"Indeed," he says, and Mía could almost swear that the word has a hint of a question in the word. He turns back to his papers. "Now, if you'll excuse me ..."

Mía knows she'll get nothing more out of him, and she walks towards the piano. She loves this room, even with Malvon in it. This is where Isabella makes magic, where she has filled the room with her lush voice during rehearsals and select soirées. For Mía, it feels like an otherworldly place, filled with beauty and emotion. When she runs the soft dust cloth over the grand piano, she does so carefully, almost reverently, following the carvings on the music rack and the contours of the shapely legs. She gently pulls the piano bench back from the keyboard, and one of the legs grates over the floorboards.

"Oh, for heaven's sake!" Malvon explodes, rounding on her. "How can I work here with all your noise?"

Mía is startled out of her reverence by his vehemence.

Malvon turns back to his papers and makes an exaggerated show of working. He mutters under his breath, "It behooves us to know our place."

"Excuse me?" Mía says sharply. When he doesn't respond, she asks, still more pointedly, "What did you say?" She stares at the back of his head. What is he implying? That her place is not here—either in this room, or in this country? It would not be the first time that she, or her family, have been made to feel unwelcome, but she didn't expect to be the target of open dislike in Isabella's home. She feels hot anger rising up her throat to her cheeks.

She goes to stand on the opposite side of the desk from where Malvon is sitting, so that she can peer directly into his face. "This is my place as much as it is yours. I have as much right to be in this room, and this apartment, and this city, and this country as you do."

Malvon continues methodically making entries into the spreadsheet in front of him as if she did not exist. There is suddenly no doubt in Mía's mind that Malvon was behind Immigration and Customs Enforcement knocking on her door in the middle of the night. Her pent-up fury explodes, and she bangs the flat of her hand on the desk. It has the effect of making Malvon jump, and he stares at her, startled, his pale eyes stretched wide behind the thick lenses of his glasses.

The intercom from the downstairs desk chimes. Mía glares at Malvon for another second, then she flings the dust cloth down on the desk, registering the look of sheer horror on Malvon's face as it lands next to his hand, before she turns and stalks towards the entrance hall.

"Hello?" she almost barks into the intercom.

"Mía?"

"Yes, Fausto," she says on an exhale.

"You okay?"

"I'm furious with Malvon, that's all." She makes no attempt to lower her voice. She hopes Malvon can hear her through the open door of the music room.

"Tell me something I don't know!" Fausto laughs. "I called up to say I have two visitors here for Miss Foiani."

"Who are they?"

"Mr. Tobia Rutto and Mr. Andrew Lilley."

"Isabella is lying down at the moment, but I know Tobia, so you can send them up, and I'll see what they want."

"On their way," says Fausto.

The first time Mía met Tobia was when he turned up for a

rehearsal at Isabella's apartment before a recital. He was small, rotund, and flamboyantly loud—to the point, almost, of being obnoxious. But then he opened his mouth to sing, and the full, chocolaty bass that resonated through the room made her eyes fill with tears.

When she opens the door to him now, he swoops her into an extravagant embrace and enfolds her so tightly that she squeals a complaint.

"Mía! *Come stai, mia cara?*" His exuberant Italian bounces around the entrance hall. He releases her, and looks into her eyes. At five foot five he is barely taller than her. "We have come to make Isabella laugh," he says, and gives a bellow of laughter, as if by way of demonstration. "Meet my friend, Drew—he is from England. He is the very best countertenor in the world."

Drew is as tall and pallid as Tobia is stocky and swarthy. His thinning blonde hair flops over his ears, and he gives Mía a wan smile, murmuring something she can't catch.

"Here's some Chianti," says Tobia, handing the bottle to Mía. "If we can't make Isabella laugh, then we will make her drunk!"

"Mr. Rutto!"

Everyone freezes, their eyes swiveling to the music room door, where Malvon stands, silhouetted against the backlighting, high color in his cheeks.

"Please show some respect!" Malvon says. "What is it with you people? Miss Foiani is resting, and I must ask, out of *my* respect for her, that you take your leave."

Without preamble, Tobia launches into *Wotan's Farewell* from Wagner's *Ring Cycle*.

"That bright pair of eyes
That I often smilingly kissed ..."

"No, Tobia," Mía says, "it is too loud." But she is half laughing as she speaks, and her scolding carries no weight.

"Let them refresh me today
One last time
With a final kiss!"

Tobia grabs hold of Mía and tries to kiss her, but she wriggles away. Then Tobia turns to Malvon, suddenly cold. "Just because you are a killjoy, it doesn't mean that there will be no joy in this house."

Malvon's nostrils flare.

"Open the Chianti, Mía!" says Tobia, his jocular self again.

"If you wish to stay in Miss Foiani's good favor, Mía," says Malvon, "I would urge you not to comply. Otherwise, I will feel it my duty to inform her."

It is too much, and Mía's temper flares again. "Who do you think you are to tell me what to do? I am employed by *Isabella*, not by you."

Malvon flushes a deep red. He draws himself up to his full height of five foot seven, turns on his heel, and goes into the music room. The door clicks shut behind him.

Silence hangs in the entrance hall for a moment.

"*Che culo!*" says Tobia, a note of disbelief in his voice.

"What's that mean?" asks Mía.

"An arse," translates Drew mildly.

"Who is he?" demands Tobia.

"Malvon Steward," says Mía. "Isabella's accountant. He thinks he's the most important person in her life, and he always acts as if he knows more about her—and anything—than anyone else."

"*You people*," mimics Tobia, enacting a mincing impersonation of Malvon.

"And 'you people' means anyone who is not like him," says Mía.

"Aha! *Xenofobo*, no?"

"Yes. I had ICE knocking on my door in the middle of the night, and I swear Malvon was behind it."

"Then he must be taught a lesson."

"Don't put ideas in my head!"

"But of course. Something that will show he's *idiota*. Let's drink to it!"

Mía says, "I don't want to agree with Malvon, but it is true that Isabella is lying down. She's been trying to shake a headache all day."

"Still in mourning for her brother?"

"It's partly that, but it's also partly ..." Mía weighs whether to say anything further. Tobia is not the most discreet of men, but he has known Isabella longer than she has. "This guy came over on Friday to talk to her about a new opera by Orson Carradine," she says, "and she's been on edge ever since then."

"Orson Carradine is writing a new opera?" asks Drew. He speaks so sporadically that Mía keeps forgetting he is there.

"That's what Isabella says."

"Will she sing in it?" asks Tobia.

"She won't say. But she's been—I don't know—restless ever since he came."

"It is time she sang again. It's been too long."

"I know. But she must be left in peace for now."

Tobia stands and looks at Mía with his feet planted wide under his stout body, and she wonders if she's going to have trouble with him.

Then he says, "*Va bene.*" He drops his voice and whispers close to her ear. "Let us know about your plan for the *xenofobo*!" His parting shot is, "Tell Isabella remember us—Drew needs work while he is in the country."

Mía closes the front door behind them, and listens for the ping of the elevator. She wonders if she should go back into the music room to retrieve her dust cloth, but she decides she'll give Malvon a wide berth.

SEVASTYAN

SEVASTYAN TAKES THE SILVER LINE EXPRESS BUS, then Metrorail's Silver Line into Washington's Union Station. He's already called the Ukrainian embassy, but they have no record of anyone by the name of Vira Blyzinskyj, so there is no point in trying to find his way to the embassy building in northwest Washington. His plan now is to head north into Baltimore to try to make enquiries at the Peabody Institute there. He remembers it's one of the music conservatoires where Vira dreamed of studying, and he's banking on the off chance that she's been in touch with them.

When he gets into Union Station, instead of transferring immediately to the MARC commuter train that will take him up to Baltimore, he hoists on his backpack, which is weighted down with his computer equipment, and wheels his bag through the grand high-arched interior of Union Station, hoping to be able to get a view of the Washington, D.C. skyline. He stands on the steps in front of the Beaux-Arts façade, looking down towards the dome of the United States Capitol where it gleams in the morning light. Over to his right he can just make out the top of the obelisk of the Washington Monument. It gives him an existential feeling to see with his own eyes these landmarks that have become such symbols of power—but also, he thinks, of conflict.

He turns away to make his way back to the dim railway platforms again to board the MARC train, hearing around him American voices and trying to translate the snatches of conversation into Ukrainian. The whole commute from the hotel to Baltimore takes him almost three hours, tacked onto the day and a half of yesterday's intercontinental transit, and in everything he does there's the shrill note of worry about Vira, like a car alarm that is never turned off.

It is entirely her drive that has brought them here. Although her demeanor suggests diffidence and reticence, he knows the intense tenacity hidden underneath. When they were children, and they used to go with their father to the instrument factory in Lviv where he worked, they'd hang out amidst the wood shavings and the smells of wood and glue, playing around on the banduras, basiolas, mandolins, and guitars. And it was Vira who stuck with the bandura and became proficient. After the accident, with their mother gone and Sevastyan undergoing one surgery after another for his back, Vira had sought out a cello teacher and gone on to win a place at the Lviv Conservatory, showing the kind of grit that seemed entirely at odds with her reserve.

Then there was that evening one June, when they were both still undergraduates, and their father had taken them to hear an early music ensemble on tour from America. At the intermission, Vira was alight with excitement—about the performers, about their viols, about their historical performance practice.

"It's like the viola da gamba has a beautiful secret, and it wants to share it with you," she'd said, "and *only* with you."

When Vira made the transition from cello to viola da gamba—adjusting seamlessly to the additional strings, the moveable frets, the different ways of bowing and holding the instrument—Sevastyan understood immediately why it spoke to her. The warm intimacy of its timbre is an extension of her quietude, just as his shift from applied mathematics to quantum computing is a reflection of the precisely logical and linear way that his own mind works.

Watching the passing Maryland landscape through the slightly grimy window of the MARC train, Sevastyan registers that he's thinking about their joined lives in the present tense, as if he will reach his destination and resume the day with her. But those days have been upended since the first case of COVID-19 was reported in Lviv. Within two weeks, their father was hospitalized. How had he contracted the virus, working alone in his instrument shop all day? They would never know. They weren't allowed to visit him. They couldn't be with him when he died. After, sitting outside the hospital under a pine tree, their shoulders pressed together, they tried to grasp that they were sudden orphans, to absorb how completely their lives had been disrupted.

"I want to go away," Vira said, blurting it out like a jagged phrase of music.

Sevastyan turned to look at her set face, seeing reflected in it the naked disbelief and bewilderment that he felt at finding themselves adrift—no parents, grandparents, uncles, aunts, cousins.

"I want to go and study viol in America." She turned her green eyes on him, slightly dilated from shock. "You must come, too. We will go together."

It was impossible, of course. The whole world was shut down. But Sevastyan, who was used to Vira's singular focus and concentration on her music, watched that focus being directed towards her search for music schools in the States that offered advanced degrees in historical performance practice: Eastman School of Music . . . San Francisco Conservatory . . . Juilliard . . . Oberlin . . . Peabody . . . she scrupulously investigated them all.

She was also unwavering in her determination that Sevastyan would share this venture with her. For every advanced degree in historical performance practice she researched, she sought out a geographically corresponding graduate program in quantum computing. She set him to find out everything he could about the kind of visas they would need to study abroad. For Sevastyan, this was like trying to find the point between 0 and 1 in a probability theory, and he set the process in motion, even though the embassies were closed. Gradually, as the pandemic began to show sporadic signs of loosening its stranglehold on the world, what had been Vira's abrupt, improbable dream outside the hospital under a pine tree seemed to be edging its way towards a possibility.

Then came the invasion. And every plan, no matter how meticulous, became meaningless overnight. At first, it had looked as if they might be safer in Lviv, in the western region of the country near Poland, but it wasn't long before the whole of Ukraine was reverberating with the chaos and the calamity of war.

At Baltimore Penn Station, Sevastyan asks at the central information desk about somewhere to store his bag and for directions to the Peabody. The large, chatty woman tells him to "take the purple line on the Charm City Circulator over on St. Paul's Street, hon," pointing in the direction he will need to go. She presents him with a bus schedule. "It's just four stops south to Centre Street, and you can walk from there to Peabody." She spreads the map out on the counter with her plump hands and points out with a long, ornately manicured fingernail the route he will walk—west a block then north a block—from the bus stop to the Peabody Institute. Sevastyan thanks her, warmed by this friendly interchange with his first Baltimorean.

"You're quite welcome. You be safe," she tells him.

When he dismounts from the Charm City Circulator and turns the corner onto Charles Street, as instructed, he is faced by a tall Doric column with a statue mounted on top. Closer inspection tells him that it is a monument dedicated to George Washington by the State of Maryland. On one of the corners adjacent to the monument, the Peabody building suggests a Renaissance style with its molded columns, pilasters, and pediments. Inside, he is directed to the administrative offices, but, as helpful as they try to be, they have no record at all of a student named Vira Blyzinskyj, either current or pending.

The let-down at drawing a blank is so overwhelming that it makes him realize how much he has been pinning his hopes on finding a link to Vira here. He is disoriented, and needs to regroup before he starts the search at refugee and immigrant organizations. He hoists his computer case onto his back again and leaves the conservatory, wandering without direction around the small parks of Mount Vernon Place. When he steps off a sidewalk to cross the street, a hand shoots out to grab his arm and pull him back, as a car, its horn blaring, passes inches in front him—so close that he can feel the momentum tug at his clothes.

"Боже мій!" Sebastian mutters out loud in shock.

"He drove straight through the red light," says his rescuer.

"I should have looked. I'm sorry. Thank you." The words spill out in a rush as if they are trying to keep up with the adrenaline shooting through his body.

"It's okay. No worries."

Sevastyan shakes his head trying to rid himself of the shock.

He takes an uneven breath and exhales sharply, then gives a short laugh—mirthless, embarrassed. "It is only my second day in America," he says, "and I'm nearly finished right at the beginning."

"The way some people drive, we could all be killed every day." Sevastyan hears that his rescuer is a foreigner like himself, and it strikes him as bizarre that they are conversing in a language that is not the native tongue of either. The man is about his own age, small and compact, probably Latino.

"Well ... thanks again," says Sevastyan.

"Sure." His rescuer steps into the pedestrian crossing and walks away.

Sevastyan waits a moment, still trying to calm his jangled nerves. He looks right, left, then right again. He double checks the traffic light and tentatively starts to cross the road, following behind the man who pulled him back. On the other side of the road, as the man turns right along the sidewalk, Sevastyan quickens his pace to catch up with him.

"Excuse me," he says as he draws abreast.

The man glances quickly at him, as if startled, and then slows his step. "Yes?" he says.

"Is there café near here?"

"I work there," the man says, indicating a brick face building with bow windows and a sign advertising coffee, tea, and light food.

"Oh!" Sevastyan grins at the serendipity of this. "Thanks."

As he walks into the café with his rescuer, Sevastyan says, "Thanks again for what you did back there."

"It was nothing."

"What is your name?"

After a beat, "António."

"I'm Sevastyan."

"Where are you from?" António asks, walking behind the long counter as Sevastyan takes a seat on a high stool.

"Ukraine."

"*Jesús!*" António exclaims in Spanish, breaking off from signing in at the till. His near-black eyes meet Sevastyan's. "They said on the news all the men your age had to stay to fight."

"Yes, that is so," he says". But I have medical—" he can't think of the English word for звільнення.

"Excuse?"

"Yes, maybe this is the word," says Sevastyan. Apart from the friendly woman at Baltimore Penn Station, it feels as if he hasn't spoken to anyone in days, and his bottled-up tension strains for an outlet. "I can come because of that, and I must find my sister. She came to America with program called Uniting for Ukraine. Then suddenly she stopped texting. One hour texting, next hour nothing. I do not know what has happened to her." It's a relief to be articulating, even in a foreign language, everything that has been wearing down a repeating groove of worry in his mind.

"This is terrible," says António, looking at Sevastyan intently.

"Yes. It *is* terrible because it is just her and me now. Our mother and our father are dead. We cannot lose each other."

"You have asked at your embassy?"

"They know nothing. I was at Peabody now because she is musician," he jerks his head in the direction of the conservatory, "but also nothing there. I will try next at refugee and immigration places."

António's dark eyes, which have been fixed on Sevastyan, flick away at the mention of these places. After a moment, as if remembering why he is here, he says, "What can I get you?"

Craving to replicate the taste of home, Sevastyan says, "Please, can you make me cold spiced tea with honey?"

VIRA

"COME AND LISTEN TO THIS, SEVASTYAN!" says Orson, without greeting, when Vira walks into his music room at the conservatoire the next day.

He opens his laptop and clicks on an MP3. The plaintive timbre of a tenor voice, accompanied by a viol consort, fills the room. Vira stands, caught in a web of sound that is at once familiar and unknown.

Who likes to love, let him take heed!
And wot you why?
Among the gods it is decreed
That Love shall die.

"Do you know it?" Orson asks, projecting over the music.

The music is so half-recognizable that Vira hesitates before she shakes her head.

"It's one of William Byrd's songs."

"Oh yes," she says. She understands now why it is so familiar. "I have played viol fantasias written by him."

And every wight that takes his part
Shall forfeit each a mourning heart.

The track comes to a stop and Orson clicks off the MP3, but the poignancy of the music stays with her.

"Shakespeare must surely have heard Byrd's music since they were both hanging around London at the same time." Orson speaks quickly, lightly. Vira feels she is beginning to recognize his various moods, and this is his enthusiastic, ebullient one. "I've been listening to this song all morning," he says. "It's my latest, best thing—how do you like it?"

"It makes my heart sad," she says, "as love songs are meant to do."

Orson studies Vira in the silence. "You said that with a bit of a pang. It sounds as if you speak from experience."

She doesn't reply.

"Well, do you?" he presses.

"Little bit."

"So, you also have 'a mourning heart' like me?"

The little experience she admitted to is unfamiliar territory for her. She pours so much of her emotional energy into music, and her bond with Sevastyan has always been so sustaining, that she hasn't felt the lack of a love interest. She had a short-lived crush on her musicology professor, but that was about it. This fluttering, jumpy, breath-snatching feeling she has in Orson's presence is a novel experience for her. It's uncomfortable and unnerving, and she would rather be without it.

"Tell me about her!" says Orson.

She almost laughs out loud at his supposition about the gender. She glances at Orson's face—the dark pools of his eyes, his high cheekbones and slightly snub nose, and the brown curls that twist onto his forehead. "She has eyes so dark it is like you are looking into water at night," she says, adopting the same pronoun Orson used, "and strong cheekbones," she touches her own to demonstrate, "and curly brown hair."

"What happened?"

Vira shrugs, gives her head a small shake, and looks away, wishing the conversation would change direction.

"Dead end, right? Like Isabella and me," he says. "So, what did you think of her?"

"Isabella is beautiful," she says, glad to grab on to a new subject, "and I think little bit sad."

"Did you make any headway with her?"

"Headway?"

"Did she agree to sing Olivia?"

"Oh. She said..." Vira tries to recall the exact phrasing Isabella used, "she said she will not commit to anything, but if I go again and take my instrument, she will read through the aria with me."

"That's fantastic, Sevastyan! Great job. When can you go?"

"I can go tomorrow," she says. "But what if she still says no?"

"If she said she'll read the aria with you, I won't accept *no* for an answer from her now."

"There is something—some sadness, or some reason we do not know—that stops her from singing. I think it will not be right to make her do this if she does not want to."

Orson frowns at her, saying nothing, and she can see the muscle jump in his jaw as he clenches it. With Sevastyan, she only needs to hint at something for him to intuit her meaning. This is more complicated. Orson wrote his opera for Isabella, just as he wrote *The Venus Hottentot* for her, and he wants so urgently for her to sing it, that he can't imagine why she wouldn't want to do so. Vira doesn't know how to make Orson empathize with the undercurrent of melancholy that she has seen in Isabella; to make him understand that it's something in *her*—not in his opera—that holds her back.

"If you told someone that you did not want to do something," she says, "you would want that person to accept it, I think."

"But, if that were the case, I would give a valid reason."

"Perhaps . . ." She doesn't know how to frame her thought.

"What?" Orson sounds quite sharp, his mood shifting, and Vira wonders if she has gone too far. She's not quite sure why she feels the need to come to Isabella's defense, except that she keeps seeing in her mind's eyes the way that Isabella turned her head away to hide her tears.

"Perhaps she cannot say."

"She's the most articulate woman I know!"

"But perhaps it is something hidden." She tries again. "I know someone . . ." She stops.

"Well, what about this someone?" he prompts irritably.

Vira shrugs. "It doesn't matter."

"Go on!"

She hesitates. Then, not looking at him, she says, "She had secrets, and she wanted, very much, to tell them. But there were reasons why she could not talk about this. And the more she held her secret, the bigger it got, until it was not possible to share it ever. And she had to go on, day after day, feeling more sad and more mixed up, but she just had to keep on doing it."

She studies his scuffed shoe with the lace starting to come untied. She wants to say more, to come clean, to confess...

Orson asks, "So, what happened to her?"

"Nothing. She pretended to be fine, even though she was unhappy inside." She pulls in a deep breath. "Anyway," she says,

"I will go and read through the aria with Isabella tomorrow afternoon, if you want."

"Of *course* I want you to go! And you can play through this one with her, too," he says, taking a heavily marked manuscript from the pile on top of the piano. "I worked on it yesterday, when my mind was full of William Byrd."

Vira reaches for the manuscript but he holds on to it. "Wait! I'll make a clean copy for you to take. This is the only one I have."

He sits at his cluttered desk, and starts transcribing the music onto a clean page. His hand moves precisely as it makes the patterns of notation across the staves, his face almost fierce with concentration. She knows that he is oblivious to her, and she studies him, taking in the utter absorption packed into his taut, wiry frame as the music plays out in his head.

MALVON

MALVON STEWARD LETS HIMSELF INTO HIS APARTMENT with his latchkey and closes the door carefully behind him. He clicks up the safety catch on the lock, turns the key of the deadbolt, and slides the door chain into its slot. Then he places his keys in their holder on the hall table, puts down his briefcase in its space between the wall and the table, and checks the answering machine. No messages. He opens the hall closet and hangs up his jacket, replacing it with the hunter green cardigan he keeps on the adjacent hanger.

He goes into the kitchen and pours himself a small glass of semi-sweet white wine. He powers up the computer on the kitchen table so that it has time to get going while he prepares his dinner. From the freezer he removes the pre-prepared Chicken à la King meal that he always has on a Monday. While it is cooking in the microwave, he lays out a placemat and cutlery next to the computer, and he folds a paper serviette into a triangle, placing it in line with the fork on the left.

When the microwave dings, he takes down a plate from the cabinet next to it. He carefully tips the Chicken à la King on the plate, scraping every last morsel out the corners of the plastic container with the serving spoon, and carries the plate and glass of wine over to the table to sit down. He shakes out the folded paper serviette and tucks it into his collar above the bowtie. He sips his wine, takes his first appreciative mouthful of Chicken à la King, and then turns his attention to the computer to check for emails.

Methodically, he starts deleting all the spam. When he sees Isabella Foiani's name in his inbox his heart jumps against his ribs. She has never before sent him an email.

For years Malvon worshiped Isabella Foiani's voice from afar, and when a tenuously mutual acquaintance happened to mention that she could do with an accountant to get her chaotic affairs in shape, it had taken every ounce of Malvon's courage, and many days of painstaking writing and rewriting, for him to craft a letter of application to her. It seemed that the idea of an accountant had been only a half-hearted idea, and Isabella wasn't seriously looking for anyone. Malvon was the only applicant, and she said he might as well try to see if he could create order out of the disarray of her administrative life.

Malvon was slightly disconcerted, when he first met her, to discover that Isabella was of mixed race. Judging by her singing voice, he had conjured up an image of an angel or a Madonna, with golden hair, blue eyes, and an ivory complexion. He couldn't reconcile his preconceived idea with this black-haired, gray-eyed woman whose skin was the color of nutmeg. He considered withdrawing his application to do her accounts. But, he argued with himself, her extraordinary musical talent outweighed the double disadvantage of having a foreign father and an African American mother. It wasn't her fault, after all, that she had been born to such parents. After wrestling with the problem for a few days, he determined that he was broadminded enough to overlook her heritage.

He was so successful at overlooking it, in fact, and he found her so beguiling in person, that it wasn't long before he was as besotted with her in person as he had been with her recorded voice. Now, his weeks revolve around the Mondays and Fridays that he spends at her apartment, and the days from Monday to Friday drag like a prison sentence.

The email reads:

Dear Malvon,

I want to tell you how much I apreciate everything you do for me. I look forward to the days that you come, and I really liked the blue and yellow tie you wore the other day. Yellow really suits you. Thanks again for everything and I look forward to seeing your smile again soon.

Your,

Isabella

He reads it once more. And then another time. His eye keeps getting snagged on the missing "p" in "apreciate." This is not a mistake that he would have thought Isabella might make. He also can't help noticing the repetition of "really" in "really liked" and "really suits." And the way "thanks *again*" and "your smile *again*" recur in the same sentence. But perhaps she just dashed off the email quickly and sent it without proofreading it.

"Dear" Malvon. Not "Hi" Malvon, but *Dear* Malvon. "I look forward to the days that you come." So, he is not the only one who looks forward to his Mondays and Fridays at her apartment. "I really liked the blue and yellow tie you wore the other day." That bow tie was part of a buy-one-get-the-second-one-half-price deal. He must go back this weekend to see if he can find any other bow ties featuring yellow. "I look forward to seeing your smile again soon." *Again* soon? Has he ever smiled at her? He is self-conscious about his smile because one of his upper incisors overlaps the other rather markedly. But he must have smiled at her at some point. She must not have minded about his teeth. He will make a point of smiling at her going forward. "Your" Isabella. Did she mean "Yours," but in her haste forgot the final "s"? Or is she trying to tell him something? *Your* Isabella. Suddenly his heart is beating very fast. Could it possibly be that she returns his feelings?

He immediately hits the Reply button. But then he stops to reconsider. He is wary of the written word. Once it is out there, it is out there, warts and all—like her misspelled "apreciate." He longs to write back with alacrity and pour out his feelings for her. But he knows that this is not the prudent thing to do. He must force himself to bide his time. *I will be a little elusive*, he thinks, *and that will make me all the more alluring to her.* He will be able to *show* her on Friday that he has received her overture, and is responsive to it. In fact, he decides with a flourish of recklessness, he will surprise her on Wednesday, and go in especially, midweek, to speak with her then.

He takes a sip of wine. Then he picks up his fork and takes another mouthful of the now-cold Chicken à la King.

VIRA

WHEN VIRA PRESENTS HERSELF with her viola da gamba at the
front desk of Isabella's apartment block, Fausto looks at her with
a mixture of wry amusement and exasperation, and says, "Yes,
Sevastyan, this time you are expected. You may go up."

The elevator pings on Isabella's floor, and when Vira steps out
onto the landing she finds the front door of the apartment already
ajar with an air of inviting her in. There is a jumble of voices and
laughter coming from inside. This is unexpected. When she had
come the first time, there had been an almost sepulchral air of
muted restraint to the place. She raises her hand to the knocker,
and the door is almost instantly thrown wide open. Mía, her face
still alight with laughter, ushers Vira inside.

The entrance hall is crowded. Isabella stands a little apart,
silhouetted between the pocket doors of a room adjacent to the
one where they met the last time. A small, rotund man with an

un-English accent is in the middle of some boisterous story, and a tall, insipid-looking man hovers nearby.

The rotund man breaks off. "And who is this?" he booms in a voice that is at odds with his stature.

Isabella says, "This is Sevastyan—I'm sorry, I don't know your last name."

"Blyzinskyj," says Vira.

"Sevastyan Blyzinskyj!" says the rotund man. "Russian?"

"No!" Vira vehemently doesn't want to be confused with the people who invaded her country. "I am Ukrainian."

"Aha! Made your escape, did you?" he remarks.

Vira can't think of anything to say in response, overwhelmed by this loud little man.

"Is that a cello?" he demands, his eyes on her instrument case.

"Viol."

"A viol player from Ukraine, eh?" He looks Vira up and down in a way that makes her feel exposed, as if her pretense of being Sevastyan is being peeled away by his eyes. "What interesting people you know, *cara* Isabella." He eyes Vira for another moment, shrewdly, calculatingly, then his face becomes affable again, and he says, "Well, I'm Tobia Rutto, and this my good friend, Drew Lilley, who is from England. So, with my darling Isabella from America, and *cara* Mía from Colombia, we have the United Nations here." He laughs uproariously, the sound seeming to ricochet around the small entrance hall.

Vira's ear catches Drew Lilley's name, and she looks at him with interest. She knows his recording of Baroque arias for countertenor, and she can't quite reconcile that exquisite singing voice and musicality with this nondescript man. *We are none of us what we seem*, she thinks, acutely aware of the irony.

Isabella says, "Sevastyan and I are going to read through some music."

"Ah!" says Tobia, his flexible voice putting a range of meaning—curiosity, intrigue, speculation—into that one syllable. "Anything to do with Maestro Orson Carradine's new opera?"

"We're simply reading through some music," says Isabella, her face and voice conveying nothing.

Tobia looks from Isabella to Vira and back again. "Well, maybe Drew and I can join you."

"Not today, Tobia." Isabella's tone is amiable but firm, and Vira marvels at her social dexterity.

"Ah well, another time, then," Tobia concedes. "Come, Drew! We will leave *la bella* Isabella and young Sevastyan from Ukraine to their music."

He kisses Isabella on both cheeks, Drew murmurs something unintelligible, Mía closes the front door behind them, and, as if a radio has been clicked off, the entrance hall is suddenly silent. Vira shifts the weight of her viol case across her shoulder, feeling bombarded.

Isabella looks across at her in the stillness. "The music room is this way," she says, turning into the room behind her.

It's a high-ceilinged room with two tall windows at one end, corresponding to those in the living room. The space is dominated by a walnut-cased grand piano—Bösendorfer, Vira notices—and an antique desk is set at an angle opposite the pocket doors. Along one wall are bookcases stacked with neatly shelved music scores, CDs, and books, some of them evidently collector's items with tooled leather spines. The other wall is filled, wall to ceiling, with musical posters—some of Isabella's past performances, some of signed programs and portraits. Covering the wooden floorboards is a huge kilim rug to warm the sound.

"Oh!" says Vira. Her first thought is how much her brother would love this room. Her next is how it is the exact opposite of

Orson's chaotic music room at the conservatoire. Perhaps that was some of the problem between Orson and Isabella.

"You can set your viol case on that bench," says Isabella, pushing the door closed. As Vira begins to unpack her instrument, Isabella walks over to watch.

"What period is it?" she asks, as Vira lifts her viol out of its case.

"It was built 1976."

"Oh! I thought all viols would be original instruments, like the equivalent of Stradivari or Guarneri ..." she trails off.

"There were some famous luthiers in Italy and England," says Vira, "but their viols are in museums or universities or sometimes in private collections. I can never afford one."

"Well, yours certainly *looks* original."

"It is copied after Barak Norman." Vira tries to gauge Isabella's level of interest. She seems genuinely curious, so she goes on. "He made viols in London in his shop he called Bass Viol near St. Paul's Cathedral. His ..." she searches for the word, "his special sign ..."

"His trademark?" offers Isabella.

"His trademark, yes, is very dark brown varnish, like mine has."

"It's gorgeous," says Isabella. "So simple, but beautiful."

Vira turns the viol around to show Isabella the delicate rosette design on the back. "I love this purfling."

"*Purfling.* What an odd word," says Isabella.

It surprises Vira that a word so familiar to her is strange to a native English speaker. "I think it means ... like ornament in wood."

"An inlay?"

"Perhaps this, yes."

"It's exquisite."

Vira picks up her bow and looks around for somewhere to sit.

"Sit on the piano bench if you like, then you can adjust it to the right height for your viol," says Isabella. "I'll just read over your shoulder."

Vira places Orson's two pieces of music on the piano's music rack. She pushes the bench a little back from the keyboard and sits, taking the viol between her knees. The height of the piano stool, it turns out, is perfect. She tightens the hairs of the bow, and tunes her instrument quickly. After glancing at Isabella to make sure that she is ready, she launches into the introduction to the William Byrd-inspired piece that Orson gave her yesterday, and which she's been assiduously ever since.

When Isabella comes in with the melody line, her tone is muted, even though she is not wearing a mask. She is not singing with full voice as she would in an opera house or concert hall, but it is the unmistakable, silken texture that Vira remembers from the CD. She feels the hairs rising along her arms—partly from the beauty of it, partly from the eerie feeling that she is in this room, actually accompanying *this* voice that she has only ever heard before on a recording.

When they finish playing and Vira looks up from the music, she finds Isabella's eyes fixed on her. "Your playing is extraordinary," says Isabella.

"Oh no!" Vira exhales on the words, trying to brush the compliment aside, feeling inadequate in the company of such an artist.

"Truly," insists Isabella. "It is astonishing the warmth and beauty you get from the instrument."

"It is Dr. Carradine's music . . ."

"No, it's not," Isabella smiles to soften the contradiction. "Sure, Orson writes interesting music, but the way you play it is exquisite."

"Thank you," Vira murmurs. "This is big compliment from someone like you, Miss Foiani."

"Oh, please, you must call me Isabella."

Vira smiles, but doesn't dare try out the name yet. "Do you want to play it through again, or shall we try the other piece?" she asks.

"Let's have a look at the other one." Isabella looks over Vira's shoulder at the music on the stand. "D-flat major, Orson's favorite key." She hums the opening melody to herself. "Hmm, this modulation to the relative minor looks as if it might be a bit tricky." She lifts the piano lid and picks out the notes on the keyboard, singing almost under her breath. "Okay," she says after a few bars, "let's give it a try."

Again, as when she first played it through with Orson, Vira feels almost as if she has to hold her breath as the musical phrases touch and skirt each other, then blend and interweave. It had been beautiful when Orson played the vocal line on the piano; now, as Isabella begins to sing out, her voice interlacing with the viol line, warming it, the music seems to yearn before it finds resolution in the final chord. As the chord fades, there is absolute quiet in the room. Vira drops her left hand from the fingerboard and rests her bowing hand on her thigh, sitting perfectly still, not wanting to break the moment.

"Well," Isabella's voice comes from behind, "Orson has outdone himself this time." Isabella's hand drops lightly onto Vira's shoulder.

"He wrote it for you," says Vira.

"But you played it for me."

"I only played his music."

"Oh Sevastyan..." Isabella pauses. Vira feels the warmth spreading under Isabella's hand. "I don't think you understand the gift of your musicality. You play this unusual instrument with great skill—but it is more than that. The instrument is just a conduit for what you have inside you ... that stirs something inside *me*."

Not wanting to be rude, but uncomfortable under the touch of Isabella's hand on her shoulder, Vira shifts on the piano bench and is relieved when Isabella takes her hand away. Vira glances back at her. "Will you sing the opera for Dr. Carradine?" she asks.

"Oh, I wish you wouldn't keep talking about him!" says Isabella. "I'd much rather talk about working up a recital with you—there's such a wealth of early music repertoire."

Isabella's suggestion is so completely in opposition to her mission for Orson that Vira feels momentarily disoriented, as if she's been playing one piece of music and Isabella has been singing another in a completely different style and tempo. She is here at Orson's behest, and everything she has done—talking passionately about the music, playing to her best ability—has been to try to persuade Isabella to sing for him.

After taking a moment to collect herself she says, "That would not be right. I ... I am here to speak for Dr. Carradine. I cannot take something for myself instead."

Isabella seems about to speak, but then she turns to look out of one of the tall windows, her profile sharp against the light. Vira stands and walks over to put the viol back in its case. Playing through music, it seems, is over. She's failed in her mission for Orson.

Suddenly, from the window, Isabella asks, "How do you perceive me?"

Vira stares across at Isabella, disconcerted by her abrupt question. She would never ask such a personal question, especially of someone she barely knew. Isabella's face is in shadow where she stands, her profile still silhouetted against the window. There is something so vulnerable about the way she is holding her body that it makes Vira feel as if she must *try*, at least, to formulate some sort of answer.

"I think..." she ventures, "I think you have unique voice. You sing like no other." Isabella remains absolutely still, as if waiting, the cloud of her hair framed by the light, the sun reflecting on her simple, dove gray dress, her slender body held taut underneath it. Vira weighs her words before she adds, "I think perhaps there is something sad in you."

Isabella turns from the window. Her mouth trembles before she bites her lips and blinks quickly, trying to dispel tears. Vira is filled with sympathy, but it is tinged with dismay.

"My brother, Julian, died six months ago," says Isabella, "and I wasn't with him. I adored him. I can't get over it." She stops. Vira feels the confidence is too intimate. She wants to break the moment but can't think how to without being brutally insensitive. "I've been so depressed and depleted, so desperate." Isabella draws in a deep breath and tilts her head back, her eyes closed. As she breathes out, she looks across to Vira. "And then you come along," she says, "with your green eyes, your fervor, your understanding, your extraordinary musicality..."

Vira feels a prickle of shock. *My God!* She thinks. *Does she imagine she has feelings for me? For me—thinking I am male.* Again, there's the sharp irony of it—especially given the feelings she has for Orson, who thinks she's male.

It is all getting drastically out of hand. And it's all her fault. She *had* to have known that pretending to be something she wasn't would end in trouble.

"I am sorry for your loss," Vira says, speaking into her awkwardness, "and I am glad if the music helped your sadness." If she pretends to be obtuse about Isabella's meaning, perhaps she can escape with no harm done. She finishes packing up her instrument, and starts walking towards the door.

"I haven't closed my mind to doing Orson's opera," says Isabella, quickly. "Come again tomorrow! I will try to make a decision by then."

ANTÓNIO

IT'S A QUIET TUESDAY IN THE CAFÉ, and António thinks that he may as well use the time to give the espresso machine a thorough cleaning. He's put the Paquito D'Rivera Quintet on low on the sound system, a student with a laptop is taking his time over a cup of coffee near the door, and a couple of young women hunch over their mugs, heads bent close together in an intimate conversation.

When the door opens, António recognizes Sevastyan.

"Hi again," Sevastyan says, sliding onto the high stool across from António.

"Hi," says António. He's glad to see Sevastyan, and realizes that he has been half looking out for him. "Did you find your sister?" he asks.

"No, and I am running out of places I can think to look. Our embassy still knows nothing. I came to ask at Peabody again and I called every immigration place in Baltimore." He says, "I can't even keep them straight in my mind anymore." He digs into his pocket to take out a scrap of paper with a name scribbled on it. "Someone at International Rescue Committee said this person, Fariba Mehta, maybe knows something, but she is not there again until Friday."

"Too bad," says António. He can feel the frustration radiating from Sevastyan. "Let me make you some tea."

"Please." Sevastyan studies his scrap of paper again. "So now I don't know what I can do while I wait to talk to this Fariba Mehta on Friday."

"You can go look at the sights—like a tourist."

"Maybe. You want to come with me?"

António shakes his head. "I keep away from such places," he says. He puts the glass of spiced tea in front of Sevastyan, glancing at him as he does so. The despondency about his fruitless search shows bleakly on Sevastyan's face. The way that he's confided his problems, coupled with the episode on the curbside yesterday and their interaction afterwards, and the fact that they're both foreigners, has made António feel a spark of connection to Sevastyan in his otherwise friendless world. He takes a leap of trust and says, "I just go between my work and my home." Then he drops his voice so that only Sevastyan will be able to catch what he says. "And hope ICE doesn't find me."

"What do you mean, 'ice'?" Sevastyan pulls his mask down enough to take a sip of his tea.

António looks across to the student by the door and the two women at the table. They all still seem preoccupied. "The United States Immigration and Customs Enforcement," he says, keeping his voice low. "I'm new in the country, like you—only I don't have the right papers."

Sevastyan stares at him for a moment as the import of this sinks in, and puts his glass down on the counter with a sharp little clatter. "How did you end up here?" he asks, matching his voice to António's.

"Little bit by little bit," António says.

"But how?"

"By boat, mainly. You know how the islands make like a half circle round the Caribbean Sea?"

"Not really," Sevastyan admits.

"Well, I come from the city of Puerto La Cruz, on the north coast of Venezuela. From there, it is not so hard to get over to Trinidad and Tobago. I stayed there a while—that was when I worked in a coffee shop for the first time. Then I found a boat to take me to Grenada. I stayed there on a cocoa farm to earn money for another boat to Barbados. And I just went on like that—working to save enough for the next boat ride, and then moving on again." He draws with his fingertip on the counter, "From Barbados up to St. Lucia, to Dominica, Montserrat, Puerto Rico—I stopped there a few weeks. Then from the Dominican Republic, I crossed the border over to Haiti, and I stayed there a while too, working in a bar at a hotel. From there, I got over to Cuba. The most difficult part—and the most expensive part—was going from Havana to Miami, but it turned out okay in the end."

"Why did you leave Venezuela?"

António checks to make sure that the other inhabitants of the coffee shop are still engaged. "I was a student at Universidad de Oriente in Eastern Venezuela near my city," he says, "and I was in a civil protest for human rights. Just once, but my name got on some government list. They came to my parents' house and took them away to question them. When I found out, I knew I had to leave quickly before I got arrested."

"And your parents?"

"They let them go that same day," says António. "My mother

is from Brazil, so my father left his job and my parents went there after I left. There's nobody else in danger. I am the only child."

Sevastyan makes a small explosion of breath and shakes his head. "It's incredible," he says. "How long were you in Miami?"

"Nearly two years, learning English, starting to be less afraid. But then a guy I was working with told me that ICE came asking about me. So then I had to keep moving again, little bit by little bit, like before. Only now, instead of boats, it was busses."

"Amazing they did not follow you."

"I thought they would. Maybe they will. But I've been here nearly six months now."

"What will you do?"

António shrugs, glancing again at the other clients. "I can't go back."

"Can you ask for asylum here?"

"It's not so easy. I need a lawyer for that, and that takes too much money."

Sevastyan glances again at the scrap of paper. "Maybe this Fariba Mehta can help."

António shakes his head. "I'm too afraid. ICE hangs around places like that."

Sevastyan lifts his glass and drains the last sip of his tea. "That was good," he says, pulling up his mask again. His green crinkle at the corners. "Some time I will teach you how to make Carpathian herbal tea like we drink in Ukraine."

António smiles in response, although he's disappointed that Sevastyan has changed the subject.

But then Sevastyan says, "I can ask Fariba Mehta for you when I go ask about my sister."

António is caught unawares by the jab of hope. He covers it with a disclaimer. "You don't have to do that for me. You don't even know me—"

"Are you kidding me?" Sevastyan interrupts, and António shoots a nervous look at the other customers in the coffee shop. Sevastyan drops his voice again. "You saved me yesterday," he says.

"Anybody would do that. It's not something like this," António says.

"Sure it is."

The student with the laptop is packing up, getting ready to leave. The two women are still engrossed in their conversation. António busies himself, removing Sevastyan's empty glass and wiping down the counter, giving himself time to think about how to respond. His instinct is to say *No*. He's afraid to do anything that might draw attention to himself. But can he really go on living the rest of his life in hiding like this? Shouldn't he at least *try* to find out if there is a chance for him to live a normal life in this country? If Sevastyan could just ask for him ... He looks up to find Sevastyan's eyes fixed on him.

"I can just ask," says Sevastyan, as if reading António's thoughts. "I don't even have to say your name."

"Thanks," António says.

ISABELLA

ISABELLA STANDS IN FRONT of the shelves of music scores with her head on one side, studying the spines. One of the first things that Malvon did, once he had restored some order to the disarray of her financial accounts, was arrange her scores in alphabetical order. He had discussed the pros and cons of the arrangement with her at great length. Would it be best, he wondered, to arrange them alphabetically, or by size, or color, or publisher? It had clearly bothered him that the alphabetical arrangement was unfortunately haphazard in terms of appearance, but he was persuaded that this ordering would be most useful and practical in the long run.

Under "D" Isabella finds what she is looking for, and takes down two volumes of the songs of John Dowland. She leafs through them. They are arranged for high voice and piano, but someone of Sevastyan's skill would easily be able to transcribe them for viol, she thinks, similar to the original Elizabethan lute accompaniment. She tucks the songs under one arm, and her eyes drift back over the music scores. She is looking for something to play to pass the time until Sevastyan arrives. She wants something clean and pure—perhaps Bach, or Handel, or Scarlatti. She lights on a collection of Clementi sonatinas. Yes, these will do.

She puts the two Dowland scores next to the lid prop on the piano, and sits down to play, choosing the *spiritoso* movement from the first of Clementi's Opus 36 sonatinas. It is just difficult enough, and sprightly enough, to keep her mind occupied while she waits. She's gone over and over the conversation from the end of their meeting yesterday, dissecting it, worrying at it. Had she said too much? Too little? What had he thought? He'd been inscrutable— not cold exactly, but not responsive either. She is not used to feeling so vulnerable. Usually, *she* is the one in control. Are her defenses down because of her grief over Julian, or is there truly something unique about Sevastyan that has so unexpectedly drawn her to him in this way? Her nimble fingers pick out the buoyant melody, while her mind continues with its feverish overworking.

When she hears the key in the front door her heart jumps, and she stops playing in the split second that she thinks it might be Sevastyan, before her reason takes over and she realizes that he doesn't have a key to her apartment. Malvon strides into the room. He has outdone himself in the bow tie department today; this one is such a virulent yellow that it looks luminous.

"Good morning, Isabella!" he almost shouts.

And then he seems to run out of the impetus that has propelled him into the room, and he just stands there, his mouth stretched from side to side in what seems to be a grin, showing his two overlapping front teeth. Mía comes to hover in the doorway with a quizzical look on her face.

"What are you doing here today, Malvon?" Isabella asks,

surprised not only that he has suddenly appeared on a Wednesday but that, after all these months, he has called her by her given name instead of the usual formal "Miss Foiani." She adds quickly, "I have an appointment soon."

"Ah!" he says. "Then we can talk later."

"Has something come up?"

"Well…" he says. "*You* know." He looks at her expectantly, his grin subsiding just a little.

Isabella can't imagine what he might believe is so urgent that he has broken his unbreakable routine and come in on an off day—she's had no career to speak of since she decided to withdraw from singing. "Perhaps there'll be time later," she says in a way that she hopes will politely dismiss him.

"Perhaps even this evening…"

She feels the sharp edge of irritation. He is being even more annoying than usual today, and she longs just to be left alone. She stares at him wordlessly, hoping that he will get the message.

"Well," he says at length, "I will be in the living room if you need me." He hovers, looking at her, continuing to grin broadly as he says, "*I want to tell you how much I appreciate everything you do for me*," enunciating carefully, as if he is quoting something profound.

Isabella looks at him blankly. Even though she is grateful that he takes care of her administrative affairs so well, she feels as if she does little more than tolerate him. Malvon gives a slight bow, and turns towards the door. Mía steps into the room to let him pass, catching Isabella's eye as she does so, and Isabella shrugs, half shaking her head. She can't think what has got into him. Mía gives a small exhalation of laughter and walks from the room.

When Isabella turns back to the Clementi sonatina, she finds that she can't recapture the pleasure of playing it. She turns on the piano bench to look out of the long windows at the sultry mid-July day. Somewhere out there, Sevastyan is making his way to come and see her. Closing the music score, she gets up to return it to its place. She glances around the room; at the upholstered bench where he unpacked his viol, the piano stool where he sat. One of the pictures on the opposite wall is askew and she crosses to straighten it. It is the original artwork for the CD cover of *The Venus Hottentot*, with the International Classical Music Discovery Award embossed on one corner.

The front door bell rings, followed by a murmur of voices in the entrance hall. Isabella turns to face the door, her heart pumping against her diaphragm. As Mía ushers Sevastyan into the room and sides the door shut behind him, Isabella registers that he is slighter than she remembered—less tall, more finely boned—but the green eyes are the same. He is wearing an oversized T-shirt with a logo on it that says *Be the Voice of the Voiceless*, and he's carrying a backpack that looks the worse for wear.

"Isabella," he says, with a half-smile.

Even though she has been waiting for him, expecting him, she feels her stomach skitter when he says her name. Does he know how effortlessly attractive he is? Or does he just go about the world oblivious to the effect that he has on people? It's his eyes, yes, but also a lithe grace that is evident despite his shapeless clothes and the clumpy boots that give him a loping walk. There's some indefinable inner quality—a combination of his extraordinary musical gift, of a warmth tempered by reserve, and a quiet surety that is overlaid with vulnerability.

"Didn't you bring your viol?" she asks.

"No," he says.

Isabella's disappointment is like a dousing of frigid water. "Oh."

"I thought we would be talking about Orson's opera—if you will do it."

116

She doesn't answer.

"You have decided?"

"No."

A silence hangs in the room. He watches her, seeming uncertain about the next step.

"I was hoping we could read through some music," she says. "I adore these John Dowland songs." She picks up the two volumes from the piano. "Why don't you take a look at them, and you can see if you could work up some transcriptions for viol accompaniment?" She offers them to him, but he doesn't make a move to take them.

"I am Dr. Carradine's..." he searches for the word, "his messenger," he says. "He will read through some parts of his opera with singers at Peabody Friday afternoon, and he wishes for you to come."

"Will you be there?"

"No."

Isabella holds the music scores against her body, wrapping her arms around them. This meeting is veering off course from the scenario she had planned when she rehearsed it over and over in her mind. She tries to rein it in.

"I'd like to get to know you, Sevastyan, and making music together—working on some Dowland, or whatever you like—would be a good way to do that." She takes a deep breath, and is mortified to realize that it's a little shaky, but she plows on. "I think I may have said too much here yesterday, but only a small part of me regrets it. You have made me feel alive again."

Sevastyan looks away from her. Isabella waits, willing herself not to fill the silence by talking too much, overstating her case.

When he looks at her again, his eyes catch the light in the room. "I am sorry," he says. "I ... I cannot explain. I am here only for Dr. Carradine ... to take your answer to him."

Isabella lets out her breath. Then she says, "Well, why don't you take the music anyway, and see what you think? Perhaps we could look over a song or two sometime."

He hesitates, but this time he takes the scores from her, swings the backpack off his shoulder, and sets it on the floor to stow the music away. When he straightens up again, he seems about to speak, hesitates, and then turns to go.

"Sevastyan..."

He stops and waits, not looking at her. What can she say to detain him, to reach him? She can't make herself any more vulnerable than she already has.

"Come again tomorrow afternoon. I will give you my answer then," she says.

He nods, and then she is alone. She leans her back into the curve of the piano, stretching her arms out along its body, her mind blank in the moments before she knows it will tumble into playing and replaying the scene, wishing for a different outcome.

VIRA

THE ELEVATOR DOORS CLANK SHUT and Vira leans her head back against the paneling, her eyes closed, trying to release the tension from her body. How much longer can she keep up this deception? She hadn't thought it through properly from the very beginning, imagining that she could just go about unnoticed and inconspicuous until Sevastyan was able to get here. Now, to add to the shrill discord of worry about him that never leaves her, her attempt at anonymity has spun out into a complicated mish-mash of twists and turns and mistaken identities, like the farfetched plot of a Baroque opera. She should *never* have allowed herself to become so spellbound by Orson's music, or so star struck by both Orson and Isabella, or so drawn to Orson the man that she wanted to try to get for him the thing he most wanted—which was Isabella.

She can't think how she can disentangle herself now from this saga that is entirely of her own making. She should just come clean and blurt it all out to Orson. She will have to own up to her duplicity once the semester begins anyway. But, as little as she knows him, she knows him well enough to imagine how annoyed he will be at having got tangled up in her deceit. She isn't ready to face that yet. Perhaps he will never want to see her again, never make music with her. Even though she finds him enigmatic and inscrutable, he's made it fairly clear that he respects her musicality, and she wants to hold on to that—at least for a little while longer. The elevator pings at the ground floor and she opens her eyes.

As she passes the front desk Fausto laughs. "She certainly got rid of you quickly this time!" he says.

Vira tries to hang on to a sliver of dignity as she pushes open the glass doors at the end of the ornate, marbled lobby. She turns right from the porticoed façade and walks north towards Peabody, starting to feel a familiarity now about finding her way around this strange city.

As she walks, she feels the rhythm of Sevastyan's name in her stride ... *Sevastyan* ... *Sevastyan* ... the way she'd heard it in the rhythm of the train carrying her away from him. If only he would come, they could explore all of this together. If only she could reach him. She aches to talk to him, to get his calm and logical insight into the mess she's got herself into, and how to get her out of it. She decides, for now, that she will come back to Isabella's apartment again tomorrow, to get her final answer, then she will put an end to that part of the complication at least. Meanwhile, today, she will have to explain to Orson that she has failed in her mission yet again.

"Sevastyan!"

She turns instinctively at the sound of her brother's name. A slight young man is darting between the passersby, running towards her. She doesn't recognize him, and the speed with which he is bearing down on her makes her flinch and take a step backwards, afraid, the memory of her attacker twisting sharply in her memory.

The man comes to a stop in front of her. "Sevastyan," he says again, slightly out of breath. "Hi!"

"Hi," says Vira, warily.

"I am glad to see you. I want to tell you something. Are you still going to the refugee and immigrant place on Friday?"

Vira feels a clutch of chill. How would this stranger know about the Refugee and Immigrant Center? How would he know the name Sevastyan? Has he been watching her? Stalking her? She takes another step backwards.

"Sevastyan?" the stranger says, his face closing a little.

"No," says Vira, whether to the name, the question about the immigrant center, or simply a blanket denial she doesn't know.

"You are not going Friday anymore?"

"No," she says again.

"When will you go, then?"

She shakes her head. Not wanting to commit anything to words in this volatile situation. People are walking past them, to and fro, along the sidewalk. If she didn't feel that she could call out to someone if she needed to, she would have turned and fled by now.

"You're not going?" When she doesn't answer, he asks, "Not at all?"

She stares at him silently, keeping her distance, wanting to turn away. But there is a sincere urgency about him that holds her there. Then something in his face shifts, like a shadow.

"If you are not going, why did you give me hope?"

"I'm sorry," she says, "I don't know what you're talking about."

He takes a step closer, and she feels a prickle of fright, but holds her ground. "I didn't ask you to do it," he says. "You offered. Why offer it if you don't mean it?"

"There is some mistake. I do not know you."

He looks stung, confused, his animation draining away.

"I must go." She begins to edge away. "Excuse me, but I have to go."

She turns away from him and walks quickly, hoping he's not silently creeping up behind her like on that night. It is broad daylight; she has felt perfectly safe when she's come along this sidewalk before. She must try to compose herself. But he had known about the immigrant center. He called her by name. How could he have known these things about her? He had called her Sevastyan ... Sevastyan. Her quick footsteps begin to slow until she comes to a standstill, people swerving around her, expelling sounds of exasperation.

He had called her Sevastyan. He had thought she was Sevastyan. If she hadn't been so full of panic, she would have realized this immediately. She spins around looking back along the sidewalk. She can't see the man. She begins to run back the way she has come, searching for the slight figure. She reaches the spot where he had called to her. He is nowhere to be seen. She looks around for a higher vantage point and stands up on the bumper of a nearby van, craning her neck.

"Hey, get off my van!"

"Sorry." She drops to the sidewalk. Is Sevastyan here—in the city? Does that man know him, and has she passed up this precious chance to connect with him? She walks around in a small circle on the spot.

"Немає!" she mutters to herself in utter frustration.

She sits down on a low wall, forcing herself to calm down, trying to think clearly and piece things together. Sevastyan must be here. He must have met that man somehow. He must know about the Refugee and Immigrant Center. If he goes there, he will surely ask about her. Fariba Mehta will tell him where she is. She must call Fariba and tell her.

Then, she will just have to be still and wait, like patience on a monument, until Sevastyan finds her.

MALVON

WHEN MALVON HEARS THE DOOR of the music room slide open, he remains where he is, seated unobtrusively in a wing back chair in the living room, waiting and listening. He has been able to make out the murmur of Isabella's and Sevastyan's voices, but he couldn't hear what they were saying. Footsteps cross to the entrance hall. The front door opens and, after a moment, closes again. That must be Sevastyan leaving. Will Mía go into the music room, or will this be his chance? He doesn't want her as an unwelcome audience again. Malvon strains his ears. He can't hear any movement. He marks his place in the small crossword puzzle book that he carries with him for moments of unforeseen inactivity like these, and he slips it back into the inside pocket of his jacket. He stands up, wincing slightly as his knees crack, and creeps towards the music room, his Hush Puppies noiseless on the parquet floor.

He finds Isabella alone in the music room with her back against the curve of the piano, her arms stretched out along its body. Were it not for the fact of her being of mixed race, she would look like an exquisite painting by John Singer Sargent. He makes his way further into the room, so that he will catch her eye. When he does, she starts upright, away from the piano, her eyes wide.

"Malvon!"

He comes to a stop, grinning at her, thrilled to hear the sound of his name on her lips.

"What are you still doing here?"

"I've been waiting for your appointment to finish, so that we can have our talk."

"I..." She stops.

He waits, full of anticipation, hardly daring to believe that this will be the moment when she declares herself.

She says, "I can't talk now. I need to go to my room. Please don't wait!"

She walks past him and out of the room. He stares after her, deflated that they haven't resolved things between them today. Now he will have to wait until Friday before he sees her again. Ah well. He takes a deep breath. He's waited this long; another couple of days won't be the end of the world.

He listens to her footsteps going up the spiral stairs to her bedroom. He knows what her room looks like; he peeked in—just once—when he was alone in the apartment. It is an inviting room with plush carpets and a tapestry on the wall over the high bed. He envisions her climbing up onto the bed and lying down. Perhaps, before too long, he will be lying there next to her. The flush that runs through him at this thought is overwhelming, and he has to clench his fists.

PETA

EVER SINCE VIRA PREPARED the cabbage rolls and potato pancakes for Peta, they have shared their suppers together. Peta is more of a baked potato kind of cook, and that's what is in the oven as she shreds some butter lettuce into a bowl and slices up a couple of avocados.

She finds the quiet comings and goings of Vira immensely soothing. There must be a thirty-year age gap between the two of them, she guesses, but there's a magnetic stillness in Vira that gives her an ageless quality. It's like the deep tranquility of the marine environment that Peta studies in her professional life. And she loves to hear Vira practice. The sound of live music in her home is an entirely novel experience for Peta, and she is bewitched by it. It begins simply and slowly with scales building higher and higher, then cycling back down again, evolving as the scales become more and more complex, until they turn into melodies that make Peta feel as if her heart is turning over.

Peta hears the key, the opening and closing of the front door, the clump-clump of Vira's boots across the entrance hall, and then she appears in the kitchen doorway. She's wearing the old T-shirt of Julie's that says, *Be the Voice of the Voiceless*. It hangs loosely on her, as do the baggy jeans. Peta tries to see her, objectively, as male, and finds that it works. Her hair is cropped short at the back with long, angled bangs that fall across her forehead. She is holding a cantaloupe.

"I saw this," she says, "and it made me think of the markets near our home in Lviv." She presses her thumbs into the opposite end from the stem, and the netted skin gives slightly under the pressure, then she holds it to her nose, inhaling the scent. "It is ready to eat tonight."

She places it on the corner of the kitchen table, wriggles her shoulders out of the straps of her backpack, and drops it to the floor near the door.

"How was your day?" Peta asks, as she and Julie used to ask each other every evening.

Vira crosses to the sink to wash her hands. "It was mixed up," she says, and she tells Peta about the stranger on the street who called her "Sevastyan."

"That's amazing," says Peta. "Do you think he could have mistaken you for your twin?"

"This is what I think also," says Vira. "It gives me hope."

She finds a chopping board and knife and tops and tails the cantaloupe. She stands it up on one end, slices it in half, scoops out the seeds of one half, and starts cutting it into wedges. Peta watches her precise, quick movements.

"It's frustrating, though," says Peta. "If you couldn't find the man again, you are still no closer to finding your brother."

"I telephoned to Fariba Mehta at the Refugee and Immigrant

Center, but they said she will not come in until Friday," says Vira. "It is hard to wait."

The oven timer beeps that the potatoes are ready, and Peta tongs them into a bowl. She gets a Stella Artois from the refrigerator for herself and pours a glass of sparkling water for Vira. She has discovered that Vira doesn't drink beer.

"Did you finish writing your grant today?" asks Vira, as she sits down and takes a potato from the bowl that Peta proffers.

It's been so long since anyone has followed her day-to-day activities that Peta takes a moment to absorb the question. "Yes," she says. "Now I'll just have to wait and see."

"It looks difficult to do."

"It's not difficult, just part of the grunt work of any research position." She cuts a cross on the top of her potato, presses the white flesh up through the opening, and seasons it with ground pepper and olive oil. "But, between constantly trying to find the funds to keep the estuary healthy and the ravages of climate change, I often feel as if I'm like a salmon battling to swim upstream."

"It is good work you do."

Peta likes watching the orderly way that Vira eats—knife in her right hand, fork in her left, as the Europeans do.

"And what about you," Peta says. "weren't you seeing the singer again today?"

"Yes."

"Has she made up her mind, finally?"

"Not yet. She says I must go tomorrow for her answer."

"Again! That will be—what?—your third or fourth time?"

"The fourth time. She..." Vira turns her remarkable green eyes on Peta, the slight furrow of a frown between them. Peta intuits that there is something worrying her, and she holds her look, silently inviting her confidence.

Vira says, "Pretending to be Sevastyan is making trouble for me."

"In what way?"

"Maybe I am just thinking this, and it is not true, but I feel that Isabella has..." she pauses to think of the word. "She has romantic feelings for someone she is thinking is man called Sevastyan."

"Could it be that she is a woman who has feelings for other women?"

Vira considers this. "I do not think this is so," she says.

"And you?" Peta finds herself asking without thinking. "Do you form attachments to other women?"

"No. I love some women," and Vira unconsciously moves her hand closer to Peta's on the table, not quite touching it, "but not in that way." She looks down at the half-eaten potato on her plate, her mind clearly not focused on it. "I have never before felt that way for a man either. With my music and Sevastyan, it was enough. But now..."

When she doesn't say anything more, Peta asks, "The composer?"

"Yes."

"And he?"

"No, nothing. He thinks I am Sevastyan." She looks up at Peta with a wan smile. "You see how pretending to be Sevastyan is making trouble for me?"

Peta traces the conundrum in her mind: the singer attracted to Vira, believing she is a man; Vira attracted to the composer, who believes she is a man. She certainly has got herself tangled up.

"What is it about the composer that attracts you to him?"

"His music," says Vira, without hesitation. "Even before I met him, I thought the music he composed for *The Venus Hottentot* was . . . was incredible."

"What's *The Hottentot Venus*?"

Vira pauses to think. "It is hard to describe. It is from poetry about a woman who lived long ago in South Africa, and she was taken to Europe and displayed in horrible ways. Orson's music, it is of Africa, but it is also of here and now. There is mixing of instruments, singer, and speaker."

"It sounds extraordinary."

"Yes. And now, hearing him play his music, playing it with him, watching him work ..." She trails off. Peta waits. "He is ... unusual," Vira goes on. "Sometimes he is excited, sometimes he seems angry. But I think this is because there is much inside him that wishes to come out—"

She is interrupted by the borrowed iPhone dinging in her borrowed backpack. Her face registers half-surprise, half-hope.

"Excuse me," she says. "May I look?"

"Of course, go ahead!"

Vira crouches next to the backpack by the door.

"It is not Sevastyan," she says. She stands, looking across the room at Peta, this time her expression is a mixture of astonishment and puzzlement. "It is from Orson."

She comes to sit down at the table again. "It says, 'Playing through the music for Curtis at my place 11 AM tomorrow. Come. Bring your viol.'"

Peta is struck by the arrogance of the word, "Come." This is a man, it seems, who is used to getting his own way.

Vira scrolls down a bit on her phone. "He has sent me map." She turns the phone so that Peta can see it. "Where is this, please?"

"Charles Village. It's not far," says Peta. "You'll be able to take the city circulator bus up from the Peabody."

Vira continues to study the phone, its light illuminating the vulnerable expression on her face. Peta thinks to herself, *This Orson had better not hurt her, or he'll have me to answer to.*

CURTIS

CURTIS BOUNDS UP THE STEPS of Orson's Charles Village row-house and rat-a-tats the knocker on the front door. He'd been so despairing about the lack of progress on the Twelfth Night project that he'd reached the point of bugging Orson about it every day, until that had proved to be entirely counterproductive. Orson can be a tricky person at the best of times, and the more Curtis pushed, the touchier and more obdurate Orson got. So, in desperation, Curtis tried a new strategy of leaving Orson entirely alone—no phone calls, no texts, no emails. It was nerve-wracking. But whether it was that or it would have happened anyway, Orson had suddenly texted Curtis yesterday announcing a breakthrough, leaving Curtis flabbergasted with relief.

When the commission first came through, he and Orson did good work together, hammering out the salient plot points in the Malvolio sequences for Orson to set to music, and Curtis is still satisfied with the way that the flow of the narrative arc hangs together. He's been working on the concept for the production with a passionately inventive designer who came up with a set reminiscent of The Globe Theatre and costumes rich in Elizabethan detail, but all shot through with anachronistic 21st century touches that give the whole design an edgy, whimsical spin. Curtis also started working on contracting the singers—with the devastating exception of Isabella Foiani. But there the project got stuck. After his initial spurt of productive energy, Orson had inexplicably ground to a halt; the result being that they can't approach instrumentalists until they know what the orchestration is going to be, and Curtis can't plan a production schedule until he knows there's going to be something to produce.

Orson opens the door and Curtis sees immediately that there is something lighter, looser about him. Orson grins—not an everyday occurrence—and, though he's dressed as usual in scruffy jeans and T-shirt, at least he's shaved.

"Come in!" says Orson. "Sevastyan isn't here, but it's not 11 yet."

He leads the way to his music room. Books and scores are piled everywhere, dust bunnies have set up home under the furniture, and the lid of the Fazioli piano, which is down, is littered with pages of manuscript.

"Just wait till you meet Sevastyan," says Orson. "He's phenomenal. He's not much more than a kid by the looks of him, but he's exceptionally musical and has an extraordinary facility on the viol."

"How did you come across him?"

"He was cleaning my room at the conservatory, if you can believe it." Orson moves some books from an armchair to the floor and indicates that Curtis should sit there. "While he was there, I sent a stack of manuscript pages flying everywhere, and when he started picking them up, I saw he was putting them back in order, so it was obvious he could read music. Then one thing led to another." He sits down on the piano bench and jogs one leg up and down in the way he does when his nervous energy is getting the better of him. "I'm going to look into a possible scholarship for the Historical Performance Department at the conservatory but, frankly, I'll be surprised if they have anything to teach him."

"Will you use him for the production?"

"Sure! He's an incredible source of information, as well as being a remarkable musician."

"I bet he's excited."

"Oh, I haven't told him yet."

The knocker sounds on the front door, and Orson goes to let Sevastyan in.

On first sight, Sevastyan doesn't look as remarkable as Orson has made him out to be, aside from arresting green eyes, which Orson had failed to mention. He's slight, medium height, and dressed in ill-fitting clothes. He stands, looking about him, as if he doesn't know what to do next.

"What did Isabella say yesterday?" asks Orson.

"She says I must go today," says Sevastyan, "and she will tell me then." His voice is light and slightly husky, with the trace of an accent.

"She's been saying that all week!" Orson explodes.

"What's her problem?" asks Curtis.

"Oh, this is Curtis," Orson says, "Curtis, Sevastyan."

"Hi," says Curtis. "Orson has told me all about you."

Sevastyan flicks his unusual eyes in Orson's direction, and then says to Curtis, "I am pleased to meet you."

"So, what's going on with Isabella?" asks Curtis.

"I think Isabella is sad," says Sevastyan, "and this is why she does not wish to sing."

"All I'm asking this time around is for her to come and hear the fricking rehearsal tomorrow!" Orson sounds really annoyed, and Curtis wonders if he is still as besotted with Isabella as he was during the *Venus Hottentot* project.

"I explained this to her," says Sevastyan.

"Oh well," says Orson, dragging his fingers through his unruly hair. "Let's play through some stuff now you're here. Just unpack your viol wherever you can find a space," says Orson.

Sevastyan does as he's told, while Orson watches him closely. When Sevastyan stands, Orson indicates that he should sit on the upright chair next to the piano bench. Sevastyan sits with his back to Curtis, and positions the viol on his calves. Orson plays a note on the piano for Sevastyan to tune his viol, which he does deftly and quickly. *These musicians are like different beings,* Curtis thinks, *with a language and skillset all of their own.*

"Let's start with Olivia's aria," says Orson. "I still only have it in manuscript. Can you see okay from there?"

"Yes."

Sevastyan plays an introduction, and then Orson comes in with the melody line. Curtis closes his eyes to concentrate on the intimate, almost muted sound of the viol. He opens his eyes again as the musical lines blend then separate, and he watches the tendons working on the inside of Sevastyan's left wrist as he moves his hand on the fingerboard. *How do they perfect these instruments?* he wonders. It seems to put them on another plane, like an athlete or a dancer. When the piece comes to its resolution, there is a moment of quiet in the room.

Then Orson says, "I liked the way you took a ritardando here before the melody comes back a second time. It prepares the ear for it."

"You didn't think it slowed maybe little too much?"

"No, actually, I thought it was perfect." Orson turns and smiles at Sevastyan.

For a split second Curtis wonders where he's seen that look, before he's transported back to the practice rooms for *The Venus Hottentot* when Orson used to look at Isabella like that. *What's going on here?* It may be that Sevastyan is a bit gender fluid, but, after the way Orson mooned around after Isabella, Curtis had always just assumed he was as straight as they come. This would be an interesting development. And, if it made him less moody, that would certainly be a plus.

"So, what do you think?" Orson asks Curtis.

Curtis pauses to collect his thoughts. "The music is so completely different from what you wrote for *The Venus Hottentot* that I can hardly believe it's by the same composer," he says. "That was rhythmic and plaintive, this is more lyrical, almost yearning."

"And?" presses Orson.

"I like it. I'm excited."

"I want it to be authentic, like *Venus Hottentot* was in its own way, but again with a contemporary edge."

"I'll need to listen to it more than once, obviously, but from what I've heard it's really working," says Curtis. "Will you have a small group of players again?"

"Not as small," Orson says, "and they won't be only one-on-a-part. I'll conduct from the harpsichord, and we'll use a viol consort—Sevastyan, you explain it to him."

Sevastyan half turns on his chair towards Curtis, his bowing hand resting on his right thigh, with the viol still supported by his legs and his left hand held loosely round its neck. "It will be consort with different sizes of viols, and you can have as many on each part as you need, like in symphony orchestra string sections. Dr. Carradine—"

"Call me Orson!" he interjects.

Sevastyan half smiles in his direction. "He is writing also special parts—like leitmotif—for each viol to go with voice of each singer, from smallest and highest for countertenor—"

"Sir Andrew Aguecheek," Orson interjects.

"To lowest violone," Sevastyan says.

"Which would be for Sir Toby?" Curtis guesses.

"Right," says Orson.

"So each of the six singers would have a corresponding viol?" asks Curtis.

"Yes, but like with orchestra any viol can accompany any voice," says Sevastyan.

"And if Sevastyan hadn't arrived to clean my room at Peabody that day," says Orson, "I'd still be messing around with modulations that go nowhere."

"No—" Sevastyan starts to protest.

"Sure!" Orson smiles at Sevastyan, and their eyes meet.

Orson breaks the moment, turning back to the music rack on the piano and picking up a sheet of music. "I want you to play through this interlude for me," he says. "It's to introduce Malvolio before the letter scene, and I need to hear what it sounds like on the bass viol."

He gets up to bring over a music stand, and he puts the manuscript on it. "Stand up, and I'll turn your chair to face us."

"I can do it."

Sevastyan moves the chair, and quickly glances through the music before he retunes his viol. Orson pushes the piano bench out into the room, nearer to Curtis, and sits down to face Sevastyan.

With the belly of the viol facing him now, Curtis hears the true, mellow timbre of the instrument. He watches the animated focus on Sevastyan's androgynous face. Orson is watching closely too, clearly engrossed—whether more by the music or the musician Curtis can't quite guess.

The moment that Sevastyan stops playing, Orson asks him, "What do you think?"

Sevastyan's eyes move over the score again, and then he says. "I like how you use Malvolio's theme again. I think it is little bit sad, but also funny where you put in syncopation."

"Any suggestions?"

Sevastyan considers. "I am thinking perhaps to use two viols for his leitmotif, playing maybe minor third apart, and see how that harmony will work? I can try to play with double stopping, so you can hear."

He plays the opening measures, and Curtis is fascinated by how much fuller it immediately sounds.

"Yes, I like that," says Orson. "Thanks, I'll play around with it." He stands up, and pushes the bench towards the piano again. "The last thing I want to go through is the accompaniment for the quartet with Malvolio, Sir Toby, Maria, and Feste. I need to hear the harmonies where the four voices come in together for the first time."

Sevastyan turns his chair towards the piano again and, as they play through it, Curtis can pick out the Malvolio leitmotif that Sevastyan mentioned. Orson is not only playing the accompaniment but, at the same time, filling in the melodic lines of the singers. Again, Curtis marvels at the skill of these musicians.

When Orson turns to him expectantly at the end, Curtis says, "I like that a lot. It's a romp, but I can hear an edge of cruelty in the tormenting of Malvolio."

"I still have to write the letter scene with Malvolio. I've kind of been putting it off because it's such a big set piece, but I think I'm feeling my way into it now."

It will be disastrous if Orson runs out of steam again. Curtis says, "Well, it's working so far, so keep it up!"

"I think it's getting there," says Orson. "Right, Sevastyan?"

Sevastyan seems taken aback to be called on and just nods.

"Listen," Orson says, changing tack, "there's an exhibition of rare, original instruments at the Evergreen Museum & Library up on Charles Street. It closes on Sunday, so we should go and see it this afternoon."

"I can't this afternoon," says Curtis.

"What about you?" Orson asks Sevastyan.

"I can go," he says.

"Good. I'll meet you there at three."

ANTÓNIO

ANTÓNIO DOES ONE MORE PULL UP on the bar he's installed over a doorway in the one-room walk-up he rents, and slowly lowers his feet to the floor. His body glistens with perspiration in the stifling humidity of the small apartment. He's been pushing himself, trying to keep his mind blank, and funneling his frustration, disappointment, anxiety into this physical outlet.

He heads to the tiny bathroom, turns on the shower faucet, strips off his shorts, and stands under the cool stream of water. He concentrates on the sensation of the water sluicing off his head and sliding down his body in swift rivulets.

Since he left Venezuela, he's made it a point to be self-reliant, to trust no one. He hasn't even kept in touch with the one friend he made in Miami, who helped him when he had to leave in a hurry. The owner of the café where he works is the son of Korean immigrants, and he's been generous; not asking questions and letting

António rent living space from him in this building. Otherwise, António has just kept to himself. Then he crossed paths with Sevastyan.

Sevastyan had eased open a crack in the shield of defense that António had built around himself, and he'd let in a thin shaft of hope when he offered to make enquiries on his behalf at the immigrant center. Since then, António has thought of nothing else; and when he saw Sevastyan on the street, he'd wanted to tell him that he had saved up a little money and could put down a deposit of sorts for an immigration lawyer. António had allowed himself to trust Sevastyan, feeling a sense of kinship in their shared outsider status in this country, but then came that cold rejection. He'd been better off before—not allowing himself to trust anyone, knowing his situation was hopeless, not opening himself up to false expectations.

António shuts off the faucet and vigorously towels his body. He knows that he'll get his self-sufficiency back and find his way into his shell again, but for now his emotions are still too ragged.

He pulls on jeans, a T-shirt, and sneakers. Before he straps on his wrist watch, he checks the time. He needs to get over to the café for his shift. Quickly, he chops up a banana and throws it into a blender with some blueberries and strawberries. He adds almond milk, agave syrup, and coconut water, then whirrs it all up. He pours it into a stemmed glass, swallows it quickly, and rinses everything before grabbing his keys, sliding his mobile phone into the back pocket of his jeans, and heading out.

It's a short walk to the café, and he knows the route to take so that he can keep mostly in the shadows—both literally and figuratively. This is his life now. He takes one of the baristas' shifts every day, goes to the store for provisions when he has to, works out at home. And that other self, the one who studied engineering at the Universidad de Oriente in Eastern Venezuela, convinced that he would change his country and the planet with his innovations, is some naïve dreamer he doesn't even know any more.

He checks his watch again. He'll be on time—just. When he rounds the corner, he sees two uniformed men emerging from the café. He steps back, flattening against the wall behind him. Had they seen him? He waits, his heartbeat thudding in his ears. There's no one else around in the heat of the day, and he just stands there, his back pressed against the building.

A traffic light changes, and cars accelerate away. António strains to hear footsteps above the traffic noise, afraid that the officers could appear at any moment without warning. He glances at his watch again. A minute to the hour. Will he have time to pick up his things from the walk-up, he wonders, or will he just have to get straight to the terminal and take the first bus out, like in Miami? Should he risk waiting to see if, by chance, the officers have gone, or should he just leave here right away?

He waits. And as he stands there, his back to the wall, a feeling of resignation settles over him like an insidious fog. For almost two years, he has avoided being picked up. But what sort of existence is this—fearful, friendless, expecting the worst at any moment? Wouldn't it be better to get it over with and be deported, rather than live on the edge of dread all the time?

No, he decides.

He waits some more, the sun baking down on him, the cicadas shrilling obliviously up in the sidewalk trees. He looks at his watch again. It's five minutes past the hour. Ten minutes have passed. Surely, they would have come by now? He steps away from the wall, and risks a quick look around the corner. The street is empty, the tables in front of the café unoccupied in the heat. He looks up and down the road. There is no sign of the men, and no vehicle with the ICE insignia on it. Have they gone back inside the café?

He pulls his mobile phone from the pocket of his jeans and calls the shop. "Hi, Jae?"

"Yes?" the owner says.

"It's António. Sorry I'm late."

"Hey, António. You okay? You've never been even one minute late before."

"I'm okay." He doesn't know how to frame the question. "Is it busy?"

"Four or five," says Jae.

"Anyone official looking?"

There's a pause. "Ah," says Jae. "No, they just came in for a couple of coffees to go. Left around ten minutes ago."

VIRA

VIRA LIFTS HER HAND TO THE KNOCKER on Isabella's apartment door, having negotiated her admittance past Fausto without problem, and realizes that she's forgotten to bring the John Dowland scores.

"Проклятий ідіот!" she curses herself under her breath. Now her business with Isabella won't be finished today, and she will have to come one more time to return the music.

Mía opens the door and smiles in recognition. "Hello, Sevastyan," she says, and then her face clouds a little. "We were not expecting you. Isabella is on the phone."

"I am sorry. She said for me to come today."

"Come in! I'll ask if she can see you."

Vira steps into the cool, muted entrance hall and closes the door behind her as Mía crosses to the music room. She can hear the low murmur of Isabella's voice coming from the room behind the pocket doors. Vira has never been alone in Isabella's apartment before, and she takes closer stock of her surroundings. Her eye is caught by a music score in an elaborate gilt frame, illuminated from above by a brass picture light. She crosses to study it, and finds that it is an autographed working manuscript of part of an aria by Handel. She starts to read the notation.

"Isabella says that she can see you," says Mía behind her.

"Thank you." Vira steps away from the manuscript and walks towards the music room. Isabella is seated behind the antique desk, with an array of papers strewn across it.

"Hello, Sevastyan," says Isabella, standing. She's wearing loose linen pants with a crisp, white sleeveless top. "I thought you were coming this afternoon."

"I am sorry, we did not make time," says Vira. "I cannot come this afternoon."

"Well, you're here now."

"I am sorry to interrupt your work."

"I'm trying to set up a singing scholarship at Peabody in my brother's name."

"Oh!" says Vira. She has come to this meeting tense and on her guard, acutely aware of the unease of their last encounter. But, seeing Isabella at work on such a poignant project, she finds herself opening up towards this melancholy woman. "This is a very beautiful thing you are doing," she says.

"I must do what I can," says Isabella.

There is silence. Vira doesn't want to trample over the remembrance of Julian Foiani, and she doesn't know how to broach the subject of Orson's rehearsal.

Isabella gives a bleak smile. "I suppose you've come for my answer about Orson's rehearsal," she says.

"Yes."

"Where and when is it?" she asks.

"Peabody concert hall tomorrow, two o'clock."

"Yes, I could make that," says Isabella.

And, just like that, she has finally given a commitment. Vira had been expecting another deferment, another prevarication, and she has come armed with so many arguments of persuasion that, for a moment, she feels nonplussed. But that's instantly replaced by elated relief. "He will be so glad!" she says.

A silence.

"Can you stay?" Isabella asks. "I'll ask Mía to fix us something."

"No, thank you," Vira says, quickly. There are so many reasons she is eager to leave—to tell Orson the news, to avoid another awkward encounter with Isabella. But, to soften the alacrity with which she said no, she adds, "I must go to Peabody. I am sorry to interrupt your important work."

"Sevastyan ..." Isabella looks down at her desk, and Vira feels a whisper of discomfort returning, afraid that Isabella will start talking about her feelings again. But then Isabella says, "I'll see you out."

In the entrance hall, Vira indicates the Handel score hanging opposite the front door. "This autograph is little bit incredible," she says.

"Julian gave it to me for my first performance at the Met," says Isabella, her eyes on the manuscript.

"This scholarship you are making in his name, it is wonderful," Vira says.

Isabella doesn't answer. Then she says, "Are you quite sure that you won't be at Orson's rehearsal?"

"I am not able."

Isabella looks at Vira with her direct, gray eyes. The silence stretches.

"I will leave you to your work," says Vira.

"Yes," says Isabella, but she doesn't move. There is a listless despondency about her. If the circumstances had been in any way different, Vira would have reached out to her.

"Goodbye," says Vira.

Isabella doesn't say anything.

Vira opens the front door and closes it behind her as gently as possible.

SEVASTYAN

SEVASTYAN IS WELL AWARE that his search is getting more desperate and far-fetched. He's come up to the Johns Hopkins University's Homewood campus on the off-chance that the graduate admissions office might have a record of an application from Vira. But, like Peabody, they have no trace of her.

Deflated, he leaves the office in the Wyman Park Building and walks along Art Museum Drive towards Charles Street to catch the Purple line south on the Charm City Circulator. Passing the museum that gives the road its name, he stops to study the neoclassical façade with its Ionic columns and pedestal. *Why not?* He thinks. There's nothing else for him to do. António had suggested he should see the sights, and spending time in a museum is as good a way as any to pass the time.

He climbs the steps and finds himself in a long, high court.

"May I use foreign student card for discount?" he asks the

attendant at the desk.

"Oh, there's no entry fee for the main galleries, Sir," she tells him. "What are you interested in viewing?"

He hadn't thought any further than trying to pass the time. "Maybe European painting?" he suggests. "Impressionists, something like this."

"Well, our Cone Wing is world famous, you know," she says, her glasses glinting in punctuation of this fact, "and we have the world's preeminent Matisse collection."

She whips out a floor plan, much as the helpful woman at Penn Station had done, and shows him where to go. At the end of the court, he turns left around a garden atrium, and he is in the Cone Wing in no time.

For an hour, he wanders between Matisse's Blue Nude and Large Reclining Nude, the Little Dancer by Degas, a cello player by Gauguin, landscapes by Monet, a Pair of Boots by Van Gogh, Picasso's Mother and Child. As he walks and stops and walks on again, he thinks of the countless times he and his family visited Ukraine's largest museum, the National Art Gallery in Lviv. He's reminded especially of the museum's Lozynsky Palace, which houses—or housed—19th and 20th century European Art. Now, all the precious artwork has been packed up and secured to protect it from the Russian invasion. As always, his thoughts cycle back to Ukraine, and to Vira.

In a side room, Sevastyan becomes engrossed in the computer generated virtual tour of Claribel and Etta Cone's apartments displaying their collection as it would have looked in their home before it came the museum. His computer brain becomes absorbed in trying to work out how the programmers recreated the moving three-dimensional images and, for the inside of a moment, he forgets the strident shrill of worry about Vira.

But it's time to return to his base and try to regroup. Leaving the cool museum behind him, he crosses Charles Street and walks up to 33rd Street and St. Paul's to catch the Charm City Circulator down to Mount Vernon. He's found accommodation in an Airbnb in someone's basement there, hoping that the proximity to Peabody may yet yield some results. Each day he continues searching ... searching ... but he's no closer to finding even the faintest clue as to what can have happened to Vira. He is staunchly refusing to allow his thoughts to take shape around the idea of having to start inquiring at police stations or hospitals. Some blind optimism convinces him that, somehow, he'll find his link to her at the music conservatoire

As the bus trundles south, Sevastyan looks out at the marble-stepped row houses that line St. Pauls' Street, and they remind him, a little, of certain parts of Lviv. All this would be an adventure, exploring the different parts of Baltimore where his searching takes him, if only he could be sharing it with Vira—if he didn't have the constant, high-pitched worry about her.

The swaying rhythm of the bus is soporific. He's perpetually exhausted from a mixture of jet lag and anxiety—on top of the confusion of leaving their devastated county. Feeling anxious and depressed is unfamiliar to him, and it adds to his sense of defeat. In the past, Vira has quasi-chided him that his optimism borders on gullibility, and his laughing response was that he would rather be gullible than cynical. Now, though, his optimism is leaching away. What is the point of anything at all if he can't find her?

At the next stop, a young couple climbs on to the bus looking wilted from the soupy humidity outside. Sevastyan's own shirt is still damp with perspiration from having been out in the mugginess of the day. Baltimore's sticky heat is like living on another planet. The hottest July day in Lviv is twenty degrees cooler than this. It's just one more thing that is alien. Everything he does in America is so entirely unfamiliar that he has to work it all out from scratch, as if he's learning to live life for the first time. He's referring constantly to the map on his phone to try to find out where he is. He's perpetually doing calculations in his head to convert one U.S. dollar to the equivalent of about thirty Ukrainian гривня. He has to examine every label in every shop to find items that would be familiar from back home. And he's doing all of this in a language that he knows well, but that is not his mother tongue.

The couple chats in low, intimate voices behind him, and Sevastyan feels his solitude acutely. António is the only friend he's made here, but *he* is living in the shadows, so afraid for his precarious status that all he knows about immigration is his dread of being detained and deported. Sevastyan's one remaining, fragile thread is Fariba Mehta at the International Rescue Committee. If that comes to nothing … he can't complete the thought.

VIRA

FOR THE SECOND TIME THAT DAY, Vira takes the Purple line north on the Charm City Circulator towards Charles Village. She will use the same stop that she did to get to Orson's apartment this morning, and then transfer to the Baltimore Collegetown Shuttle on the Johns Hopkins campus to get up to get to Evergreen Museum & Library for the rare instrument exhibition.

Each day, she adds a new experience to her slowly expanding knowledge of the city. Sevastyan would be proud of her resourcefulness, given that she's generally tentative about finding her way about. Her thoughts turn back to him in everything she does. Even when her worry for him is not uppermost in her mind, there's a nagging discomfort, like a string that has worked its way out of tune, and it's not long before her fretting starts up again. Where is he now, right at this very minute? she wonders. He's not fighting in the war, that much she knows, but how and where is he living from day to day in a country pounded with the bombardment? By a chance that seemed like a miracle, she had found the mobile number of one of their Lviv friends scribbled on a scrap of paper amongst her recovered documents, and she could hardly keep her fingers steady enough to punch the number into her borrowed phone. But it just rang and rang. She keeps trying at intervals through the day. It's the only fragile thread she has to him.

The bus passes through a few dubious blocks with boarded up buildings before it breaks through into leafy streets as it nears the Baltimore Museum of Art. With Wyman Park on her left, she stands and makes her way to the front of the bus. This is her stop. As she walks north from Art Museum Drive towards the campus, she watches the bus ride north, and turn right on 33rd Street to begin its southbound route.

ORSON

THE LATEST THAT ORSON EVER ARRIVES for an appointment is exactly on time, and he gets to the Evergreen Museum & Library at a quarter to three. He finds a spot of shade on the front steps and sits with his back to the columned façade to wait for Sevastyan to come, thinking he will see him as he makes his way up the winding road to this Gilded Age mansion. He takes out his phone and scrolls through it absentmindedly. He's not one for social media, but he finds a scholarly article that he's saved about the viol as a sexual metaphor. It uses as a jumping off point Sir Toby Belch's claim in *Twelfth Night* that his friend, Sir Andrew Aguecheek, "plays o' the viol-de-gamboys." It doesn't take much of a stretch of the imagination to gather that the sexual innuendo comes from the way the viol is held between the knees. Orson becomes engrossed in his reading, and it is only when a shadow falls across the screen of his phone that he is aware of Sevastyan standing right in front of him.

"Ah, good!" he says, unfolding his long body and looking down at Sevastyan on the step below him.

"Hi," Sevastyan squints up at him in the sun. Since he's outside, he is not wearing his mask, and he is half smiling. Orson grins back in response.

"How did you get here?" Orson asks.

"With Baltimore Collegetown Shuttle from Johns Hopkins campus."

"I can run you back afterwards, if you like."

"Thank you."

"Come on, let's get out of the broiling sun."

As they walk around the corner of the mansion to the side entrance, Sevastyan says, "Before I came, I went to ask Isabella again about your rehearsal tomorrow."

"And?"

"She says she will come."

"Finally! That's fantastic, Sevastyan. I *knew* you'd be the one to talk her round eventually."

Sevastyan just smiles sideways at him, his eyes half obscured by the angular cut of his hair.

Inside, Orson flashes his faculty card at the admissions desk and waves away Sevastyan's protest as he buys a student ticket for him. They pass through to the Far East Room with its maroon-painted wood paneling and cases holding netsuke and other treasures ranged along the sides. As they don their masks, Orson is pleased to see that they are the only ones there, so they have the place to themselves. He stops immediately at the first exhibit on the right just inside the doorway, and bends to read the information card: *This lavishly carved virginal was made in 1568, most likely in Flanders. It is painted with flowers, a characteristic of keyboard instruments made in Antwerp during the 16th and 17th centuries.*

The case is carved in the exuberant Northern European Renaissance style.

"None of these early virginals had legs," he explains to Sevastyan, "so they had to be placed on a table, like this one, in order to be played."

"Like in the Vermeer paintings," says Sevastyan.

Orson looks at him. "Oh?" he says.

"He made two paintings of young women playing virginals— one sits and one stands. He painted also, sometimes, violas da gamba."

There seems to be no end to the surprising information that is packed away into Sevastyan's compact head. They move on from the virginal to a spinet.

"Do you know about the string construction on these early keyboard instruments?" Orson asks. Evidently, he can't take it for granted that Sevastyan doesn't have an extensive knowledge of just about everything.

"No." Sevastyan looks at him with his clear, green eyes, waiting to be enlightened.

"Well, in the oblong case of the virginal over there, the strings are set parallel to the keyboard. But you see here the spinet has this peculiar, triangular shaped case, and the strings are at a thirty-degree angle to the keyboard."

Sevastyan cranes up to get a better view inside the open case. "Why?"

"To save space, I guess, and probably money too," says Orson. "It has the same plucked string action as a harpsichord, so it's really just the weird angle and its smaller size that sets it apart from that."

Sevastyan's scrutiny shifts over to the adjacent harpsichord.

"You see here," says Orson, following his look, "the strings of the harpsichord are at a right angle to the keyboard, like in a grand piano."

The light in the long room is dim, and Orson stoops again to read the information card aloud: "*This harpsichord was built in Venice, one of the main instrument-producing centers in Europe during the 16th century. The instrument has undergone a number of changes, including the altering of the range of the notes, a sign that even if musical fashions changed during the next century the prestige of Venetian instruments remained intact.*" He eyes the instrument skeptically. "I'm not sure I agree with that," he says. "I think French and English harpsichords have the edge, and German, of course."

He moves on to the next harpsichord, which is a larger, English instrument with a walnut and spruce case, and the two keyboard manuals made from ivory for the natural notes and ebony for the sharps. It takes all Orson's self-control not to reach out and sound a chord.

As he reads the information card, Orson is aware of Sevastyan's footsteps clumping over the patterned rug to the other side of the room, as if he is irresistibly drawn to the viols on display along the opposite wall. Orson turns slightly to watch him. The boots that Sevastyan favors give him a loping stride, which is almost ungainly, but is offset by a kind of lithe grace. All his clothes are too big for him, and hang unflatteringly on his slim frame. Orson wonders what his frame is really like underneath it all.

Sevastyan stops in front of a viol, studying it, shifting his weight fluidly to one leg, his head tilted the other way. As if feeling Orson's eyes on him, he looks suddenly across the room, and their eyes collide. Orson's stomach lurches. It's just the discomfort of being caught staring, and he tries to ease the moment of awkwardness by grinning at Sevastyan and walking over to join him at the viols.

"They have a John Rose!" says Sevastyan, his eyes alight.

"What's so special about John Rose?"

"There are two—father and son, and they were famous luthiers in London."

"I thought viols originated in Europe."

"You are right to think this," says Sevastyan. "But then some Italian musicians went to the court of Henry the Eighth, and they started to play in viol consorts. This is why I love English viols." As he speaks, he rests his eyes on the Rose viol with a look that Orson can only describe as reverence—the way *he* might feel about a Steinway or a Bösendorfer.

Orson reads the information card aloud: *This example is undated and is signed simply* John Rose, *so it could have been made by either the father (ca. 1530 – ca. 1597) or the son (ca 1560 – 1611), who both had the same name*—"ah yes, as you said," he interjects. *The Roses were the leading viol makers in London in their day.*

Orson looks at the card for the next viol in the display. "This one is also from England, made by someone called Richard Meares."

"He is famous also. They all had instrument shops around St. Paul's Cathedral in the 1600s. Richard Meares was perhaps teacher of Barak Norman in London, and my instrument is copied from Barak Norman."

"No kidding!"

They continue to amble around the rest of the exhibition, stopping and starting in an easy rhythm together, past the lutes and guitars, the recorders and flutes, and the curiously named crumhorn, shawm, and sackbut.

When they climb into Orson's second hand Audi to head down to the Hopkins campus, he says, "I'm reading an article about the viol as a sexual metaphor. Does it feel like that for you?"

"Please tell me meaning of this word."

"Which—sexual or metaphor?"

"I know sexual," Sevastyan says with a smile in his voice.

"Well, a metaphor compares one thing to another, but it is not a literal comparison—like at the opening of *Twelfth Night* when the Count says, 'If music be the food of love,' and so on, he's comparing music to food and love to a body that must be fed to be nourished."

"Then it is like our word, метафора." Sevastyan is quiet for a moment, as he seems to be considering Orson's question.

"So?" prompts Orson.

Sevastyan says, "It is not, for me, sexual metaphor in physical ways. I saw always my teacher hold her cello between her knees, so it was just this way for me also. And now with gamba, too." He glances over at Orson. "This is from Italian, you know?"

"You know I don't speak Italian."

"Viola da gamba is 'viol for leg.'"

"Oh, right."

"And viola da braccio is 'viol for arm,'" Sevastyan says. "For me, it is just viol for leg because it is too big to be viol for arm. It is how we hold it so we can play it for comfort, for..." he seems to grope for a word.

"For convenience?"

"Yes, for convenience. So, I do not think viola da gamba as instrument is sexual. It is *music* that is sexual—how it builds, how it rests—and when you play with others, it is joining together without words. It is close ... intimate. You can see sometimes on players' faces that it feels, maybe, little bit sexual." He half laughs as he finishes speaking, and looks quickly at Orson before turning to look out of the passenger window.

Orson glances over at Sevastyan's profile. He has so exactly described his feeling about making music, and how it can sometimes feel like a wordless act of love. If Sevastyan had come to him as his student and he had taught him composition, he is quite sure he would not have had the same intrigued response to him. It was their making music together—listening, intuiting, being sensitive to one another's breathing with the music—that had made him feel a connection to this unusual, androgynous young Ukrainian. It's as if playing their instruments together had taken the place of getting-to-know-you conversations. There's so much that Orson doesn't know about Sevastyan, but still he feels as if he can intuit something about his interiority, his sensitivity, from the way that he responds to music.

They drive on without speaking, the hum of the Audi's motor filling the companionable silence between them.

FARIBA

WHEN FARIBA WALKS INTO THE WAITING ROOM at the Refugee and Immigrant Center, she doesn't even have to call his name. He is instantly recognizable, even though he's wearing a face-mask. She walks right up to him and says, "You must be Sevastyan Blyzinskyj."

He stands quickly, looking taken aback. "Yes?"

"I'm Fariba Mehta," she says. "You're just like her."

"Vira?" The urgency in that one word says everything about his pent-up worry.

"Yes. It's the eyes, especially." Fariba smiles. "Come through to my office."

As she turns to lead the way, Sevastyan's anxiety stumbles out in a string of questions. "She has been here? Where is she, please? She is okay?"

"Well, she had a bad experience," Fariba says over her shoulder, "and she lost her phone."

"Oh! So *that* is why..."

Fariba indicates one of the upright chairs opposite her desk for him to sit. "She is staying in the Patterson Park area downtown where there is a Ukrainian community." She turns towards her computer screen to access the information. "I will give you the address and her new mobile number."

"What was the bad experience?" Sevastyan asks.

Fariba has the sense that relating Vira's attack second-hand would do more harm than good. She wouldn't be able answer the myriad questions that would inevitably follow. She meets Sevastyan's eyes and speaks gently, "I think it will be better for her to tell you herself."

He seems about to pursue it, but then he nods.

"Here are her contact details; you can put them directly into your phone."

She reads Vira's address and phone number as Sevastyan punches them in.

"Thank you," he says. He presses his thumb and forefinger to his eyes.

"Are you okay?"

"Just quick pain, behind my eyes," he says. "I have been so worriedcs, but now I know she is safe ... now the pain comes."

"On top of the strain of having to leave your country." Fariba deals with situations like this every day. Each one is unique, though the trauma of it is universal. She reaches into one of the drawers of her battered desk and hands him a strip of pain medication.

"Here is something for your headache. Help yourself to some bottled water on the shelf behind you," she says.

He unscrews the top of the bottle and pulls his mask down, revealing an even more startling likeness to Vira, before he knocks back a couple of pills. As he hands the strip back to her, he says,

"Thank you. I think Vira turned to you for help, and now I am doing the same."

"That's why we are here."

"I think there is certain kind of person who will put them self in service of others, and you are like this."

Fariba studies him, his face-mask back in place. He's clearly been sick with worry about his sister, and yet he has the capacity to stand outside himself and see another person. "You are truly welcome," she says. "Is there anything else I can do for you?"

"There is one other thing. I wish to ask about political asylum."

"Well, Vira's visa is granted under the humanitarian parole program, so she doesn't need political asylum. What is your status?"

"I have tourist visa."

"Well then, neither of you needs to go that route."

"It is for my friend."

"You can tell your friend to come and talk to us, and we'll see if anything can be done."

"He is afraid. He says immigration enforcement people hang around places like this."

Fariba knows all too well of situations where this has happened. "What are his circumstances?"

Sevastyan seems to be choosing his words carefully. "He was part of civil protests in his country—"

"Which country?"

Sevastyan hesitates.

"You don't have to worry," Fariba says. "We don't deport people here. We try to help them, if they have just cause."

Sevastyan nods. "Venezuela," he says.

"Ah yes, we've dealt with a number of political refugees from there. How did he get into the States?"

"He told me he came by many different boats from one island

to another until he got to Miami."

"Does he have papers?"

"He has his passport from Venezuela, I think, but no papers for America."

Fariba sighs. "Those are some of the most difficult cases to bring," she says. "But it's not impossible. We have a team of pro bono attorneys who represent undocumented immigrants in certain circumstances. Here," she hands him her card, "tell him to call me, and we will see if we can help him. And I'll sound out some lawyers to see if they think they can make a case."

"Thank you." Sevastyan stands. "Thank you for your help, and for Vira, too." He reaches across the desk to shake her hand.

"Just call me if you need anything else."

The phone on Fariba's desk rings and she glances at it, recognizing the number of the Afghan support group she's been chasing for days. "Sorry," she says, "I have to take this. Can you see yourself out?"

"Yes," he says, "thank you again."

SEVASTYAN

IN THE WAITING ROOM, Sevastyan sits down and immediately dials the number Fariba has just given him. It rings and rings, each ring bringing him closer to hearing Vira's voice. He never speaks on the phone in public places, but these are extenuating circumstances and he will have the semi-privacy of speaking in Ukrainian. The phone clicks over to the voicemail of a complete stranger called Dr. Julie someone-or-other.

Sevastyan stares down at his phone in disbelief. He closes his eyes and sits absolutely still while disappointment, frustration, and his headache pulse through him. The number surely isn't wrong. Fariba read it directly from the screen and, even though he is exhausted and jetlagged, he still wouldn't make a mistake like that. He feels awkward going back to Fariba's office to ask for more help when she is busy on the phone. This is just another convoluted problem that he will have to solve himself. He studies the address

Fariba gave him, and he decides to try to find his way there.

Sitting on the southbound Purple line of the city circulator, Sevastyan feels his body unwind as relief begins to jostle out the anxiety that has dogged him for so long. She is safe, his body tells him. Vira is safe. He thinks of the games of hide and seek that they used to play as children. She was so skinny and supple that she could squeeze herself into the most unlikely places, and he would invariably walk past her any number of times before he eventually found her. She is proving just as elusive now, but he will track her down eventually, just as he always has.

Sevastyan looks up the address on his phone app, cross-referencing with the now crumpled city circulator bus that the chatty woman with the manicured fingernails gave him at the train station on his first day. He changes to the Orange line, and then walks east towards Patterson Park.

As he waits for his knock to be answered at the address Fariba gave him, even knowing now that nothing fatal has happened to Vira, the worry of the past ten days beats with the seconds that tick by. When the door opens, he is faced, not by Vira, but by a tall, thin woman with spiky gray hair and piercing blue eyes.

PETA

PETA IS SURPRISED to find Vira standing on the doorstep, given that she has a key. Only it isn't Vira. "You must be Vira's twin," she says.

"She is here?" His voice is sharp with urgency.

"No, sorry. Not at the moment. Come in."

"I am Sevastyan Blyzinskyj."

"Yes, I know," she says, smiling.

"Vira is living here?"

"Yes." In the hallway, with the afternoon sun slanting in through the side windows of the front door, Peta studies the part of Sevastyan's face that is not covered by a mask—the green eyes, the pale skin, the straight black hair and the way it falls across his forehead. "It truly is astonishing how alike you are," she says.

"Only our mother and father knew us when we were little," he says, "but now it is not so much."

"Yes, Vira told me that about your parents, but when you find her, you'll see that the two of you look identical again."

"Where is she, please?"

"I think she's at the Peabody Conservatoire. She's taken a part time job there until the semester begins."

"The conservatoire! But I have phoned there so many times, and I have gone there also to look for her." He seems at the end of his rope. Peta has been living with Vira's day to day desperation about losing contact with Sevastyan, and she can't even imagine what it must be like for *him,* having had his connection to her so suddenly and inexplicably severed.

"It's just a part-time job, so they likely don't have a record of her," she says.

"I have been also trying to call her since before I left Ukraine, but now someone tells me just today she lost her phone." He proffers his phone. "I have this number here, but the voicemail is for someone else."

Peta glances at the phone and recognizes the number of Julie's old phone. "Yes, this is the right number for the phone she has now," she says. "But also, give me yours, and I'll pass it on to her as soon as I see her." Sevastyan holds up his phone, and Peta punches in his number on her own. "If you still can't find her at the conservatoire," she says, "try to get hold of someone there called Orson."

"Orson?"

"Yes. I can't remember his last name, but Vira's been doing some work with him, and she's been involved in setting up a rehearsal at the music school this afternoon. He may be able to put the two of you together."

"You have been big help, thank you."

"Can I offer you something to drink before you go?"

"Thank you, but no."

Peta pulls open the front door. "Good luck! I hope we can

meet properly soon."

"I hope this, too. Thank you."

Peta watches him walk away. Vira has not only emulated his haircut, but also the physicality of his slightly loping stride. They must know every nuance of each other these two, she thinks, for Vira to have been able to achieve such a pitch perfect replication.

VIRA

VIRA KNOCKS ON THE DOOR of Orson's room at the conservatory. Getting no response, she tries the handle, and the door opens. She is disappointed not to find him here. She has even brought her viol with her on the chance that he might want to run through some of the pieces before the rehearsal. She puts down the cleaning bucket, rests her viol in a corner, and looks around her. Usually the door is locked if Orson isn't here, and she's never been in his room without him here. She sees the room with new eyes in the freedom of doing so unobserved.

His doctoral degree is propped up on a shelf in the bookcase, kept in place by an old-fashioned, cone-shaped wooden metronome. The other shelves are crammed with piano scores, some standing, some piled on top of each other haphazardly. Vira skims the spines: *The Art of Fugue* by Bach cheek by jowl with Debussy *Preludes*. Late period piano sonatas of Beethoven,

Chopin's Nocturnes, Schumann's *Scenes from Childhood*, Clementi Sonatinas, Schubert Lieder, Mozart ... Gottschalk ... Liszt. Jammed in here and there between the music scores are some slim volumes of poetry. The CDs are just as haphazard, ranging from John Dowland to John Adams to Ladysmith Black Mambazo.

The sheet music on the piano is still neatly stacked, just as she'd left it on her first day here. She sits on the piano stool and runs her fingers up and down the keyboard in a C major scale. She'd had basic piano lessons when she was younger, but she had never warmed to it; her sense of pitch was set on edge by the piano's tempered scale. Her affinity was always for stringed instruments— bandura ... basiola ... cello ... viol.

Vira drops her hands from the keyboard, and sits still, absorbing the silent aura of Orson's messy room. This is his place. This is where he makes music—both in the literal sense of creating something from nothing, and in the practical sense of lifting it off the page and playing it. The room holds an intimacy for her because it has his imprint: the spillage of his creativity, the chaotic single-mindedness, the forthright push and energy. She should get on with cleaning the room, finishing up her shift for the day, but she wants to sit here amongst his things, absorbing his absent presence.

Orson's desk reminds her of the memory test game that their mother used to set up for the twins to play, when she'd arrange random objects on a tray, and they would study them for thirty seconds then turn away and see how many they could remember. Aside from the university issued computer, keyboard, and mouse, there's an assortment of mismatched pens, pencils, scratchpads, and notebooks; a conductor's baton; an inside-out pullover; a stapler tipped on its side; a mobile phone charging cord; an unused coffee mug with the Peabody emblem; sundry books on harmony, counterpoint, and other aspects of music theory; a black leather glove; and a scramble of pages and papers, with the curiously abstract trophy for his International Classical Music Discovery Award pressed into service as a paperweight.

Vira crosses to the desk and absently begins to pick up the various pens and pencils, arranging them in her hand so that the writing ends all point the same way, and she drops them into the coffee mug. She picks up the stapler and places it upright. She winds the charging cord around the fingers of her left hand and aligns the coil with the mug. She sorts the books into a stack at the back of the desk with the spines facing her, arranged from largest at the bottom to smallest on top, and she places the baton in line with the front of them. She does something similar with the notebooks and scratchpads, and then she starts on the jumble of loose pages so that they, like the pens, face the right way.

Given the rough and tumble of his surroundings and his appearance, his notation and his handwriting are unexpectedly beautiful. His script has a slanted, italicized order to it. Her attention is caught by two scraps of poetry written out in his hand on one of the pages.

I hear but I must never heed
The fascinating note,
Which, fluting like a river reed,
Comes from your trembling throat
— Claude McKay

And, lower down on the page, with a different pen and ink, but still in his handwriting:

...everything that touches you and me
Welds us as played strings sound one melody.
Where is the instrument whence the sounds flow?
And whose the master-hand that holds the bow?
O! Sweet song—
— Rainer Maria Rilke

Vira looks instinctively towards the door, feeling as if she has guiltily stumbled on a terrible intimacy. Quickly, she pushes the page back amongst the others into the middle of the pile. *The fascinating note from your trembling throat* ... that is so obviously a reference to Isabella. And the line, *Welds us as played strings sound one melody,* describes her own feelings about him as much as it describes his feelings for Isabella. The very first time he played his music with her, she felt a deep synchronicity that she has never experienced with anyone but Sevastyan.

She picks up the ICMA trophy and examines it. Then, as if to put a full stop to what she has learnt, she places the award on top of the ordered pages to weigh them down again.

Vira turns his pullover right side out, catching a trace of his clean, buttery smell, and drapes it over the back of the desk chair. She doesn't know what to do about the single glove, so she places it on a corner, hoping that it will call to its mate from there. As she makes headway through the random chaos, she disturbs the dust of weeks, and she deals with that as she goes.

She sits down on the desk chair, still holding the dusting cloth, and surveys her handiwork. She is pleased with it. There is something deeply calming for her in beauty and order, like when her attention catches on something as simple as the dusty bloom on a dark plum or the random formation of clouds into a sculpted mass. Part of her love affair with the viola da gamba is the sensual pleasure she finds in the gentle slope of its shoulders, the warm glow of its wood, the intricate purfling in its design. And she finds a similar serenity in order—not a rigid, stifling neatness, but a sense that some things belong together and are in harmony with each other, while others are not. Sevastyan used to keep his watches and the charging cords for his devices in the same drawer as his underwear back home in Lviv, but she could never put such disparate objects together. So, Orson's desk, as she has ordered it, is coherent—but it still, she thinks, radiates his eclectic personality.

What she doesn't understand is why she, who is drawn to order and harmony, should be so drawn to a man whose chaotic and unruly surroundings are an encapsulation of everything about him—with the exception of the way he makes music. And that is it; it's *because* of his music; the thing she had found compelling without ever conceiving of meeting him. But still, why is she so drawn to *him* as a person despite the quicksilver volatility of his moods, his abrupt, almost abrasive manner, the way that his nervous energy yanks everything along relentlessly in its slipstream?

She thinks about this, sitting here in his space, and the only answer she can come up with is that it is because every one of his traits seems to be directed towards the penetrating focus of his relationship to music. And in that he is so empathic, intuitive, and sensitive that it seems to become another piece of herself, whether she is listening to it or playing it.

She is stretching out her time in his room, half-hoping that he will come in. But he doesn't. She gets up to empty the wastepaper basket into the bin outside, wipes down a few more surfaces, picks up her viol from its resting place, and lets herself out.

ISABELLA

ISABELLA SLIDES DOWN IN HER SEAT in the darkened auditorium and props her feet in their ballet flats on the seatback in front
of her. Her linen swing dress falls loosely around her legs. The stark
rehearsal lighting on the stage picks out Orson at the harpsichord.
Drew Lilley sits to one side studying a score, and Tobia Rutto
stands with three other singers before a collection of mismatched
music stands. They are reading through the music for the scene in
Twelfth Night where Sir Toby Belch, Maria, and Feste the Fool are
tormenting the imprisoned Malvolio.

As they piece together the music under Orson's direction,
it's evident that Tobia is singing the bass part of Sir Toby Belch.
The others are Malvolio, a baritone; Maria, a contralto; and Feste,
a tenor. That leaves Drew Lilley as Sir Andrew Aguecheek. The
vocal quartet is intricate and complicated, and Isabella is fascinated
by the ingenuity of its tonal color as it begins to take shape. Orson

has managed to capture both the boisterous hilarity of the situation and the poignancy of Malvolio's plight. Isabella is aware of a new harmonic inventiveness that experiments with interweaving musical lines, skirting the very edges of tonality, while always being grounded in it. Even as she tries to push the thought away, it occurs to her that if the rest of the music is as imaginative as this quartet and the two arias she's read through with Sevastyan, she *might* be tempted to sing the part of Olivia after all. Orson's music has always sat well with her voice. No matter how complicated his chord structures, she's always seemed to know instinctively where to pitch her note.

The door at the side of the auditorium opens, shooting a shaft of light along the floor towards Isabella's seat. She glances over and feels a jolt of adrenaline. Even though he's wearing a face-mask, she recognizes Sevastyan. He's come after all. He is silhouetted briefly in the light before he softly closes the door behind him and stands still, evidently trying to get his bearings in the dark.

"Hello!" she whispers, and his head turns quickly towards her.

He gingerly makes his way to her in the dim light, and he crouches next to her seat. "They said I could find Orson here," he whispers in the accent she has come to know and love.

"He's just started the rehearsal," she says, indicating the platform. "Sit here with me until he's done."

She straightens up in her seat and moves her knees sideways to allow him to pass. He's got on different clothes from the baggy jeans and T-shirts he usually wears, and they make him a little bulkier. As he sits down on her right, his upper arm brushes hers. Aside from the time she had rested her hand on his shoulder in her music room, it's the only time they've touched, and she's acutely conscious of it.

Orson, as if aware of a small disturbance in the auditorium, turns on the keyboard bench and, shielding his eyes from the rehearsal lights, calls out into the darkened auditorium, "How is the balance, Isabella?"

"Pretty good," she calls back. "Feste could sing out more."

Orson turns back to the singers, and, after some directives from him, they begin another run-through from the beginning of the quartet. This is the second time that Isabella is hearing it now, and passages are starting to sound familiar. The quartet builds to the point where all four voices come in together for the first time in a harmonic structure that manages to be both surprising and exactly as it should be at the same time.

Isabella leans to whisper in Sevastyan's ear, "Listen for this..."

She watches him in the dark, waiting to see if he will recognize the point in the music that she is waiting for, and she notices in another part of her brain that his eyebrows are more pronounced than she's noticed before. When the four voices come in together and he nods in recognition, the shared moment gives her the nerve to reach across and squeeze his arm above the elbow where it is propped on the armrest between their seats. His head swivels slightly in her direction, as if in surprise, but then he sits perfectly still, not pulling his arm away. They sit in the dim auditorium in a little cocoon of intimacy, her hand resting lightly on his arm. He's always been so cool and standoffish with her that she was half expecting to be rebuffed again now, but he seems more responsive at this moment—even if a little on the *qui vive*. As the music starts to build to its resolution, she feels a wave of serenity, and it has been so long since she's felt anything but bleak desperation that her contentment seems to flirt with euphoria.

When the quartet finishes, Orson says, "Good job guys! Great reading, thanks." He turns on the keyboard bench towards the auditorium again, and calls out, "Isabella, I just need to run up to my room quickly to fetch another piece to play through with them. Is that okay—can you stay a little longer?"

"That's fine," she calls back. She feels as if she could sit here forever in this dark auditorium with her hand on Sevastyan's arm.

"Can I try to talk to Orson when he comes back?" Sevastyan whispers.

"Let's see," she says. "It might be better to wait until he's finished the rehearsal. His mind will be all over the place, otherwise."

They sit quietly for a few moments. Just as the silence starts edging towards feeling awkward, she says, "Does it feel—" and Sevastyan also starts speaking at the same time.

They both stop, half laughing.

"You first," he says.

"I was just wondering if everything feels very strange to you in America," she says. "Whenever I've gone on tour, I've found it challenging trying to adapt to the different customs and currency and language in a new country."

"You are right, it is challenging. With language and currency, not knowing anybody, or where to go. It is all different," he says, speaking just above a whisper. "But we used to talk often about maybe coming one day to America. And then it was the war, and it is suddenly dangerous, so my sister must leave—"

"You have a sister?"

He seems momentarily deflected, and looks at her with a question in his eyes.

"I'm sorry to interrupt," she says. "Your sister had to leave?"

"Yes," he says, "because of invasion. And she waited and waited, wishing for me to come also. But I could not at that time. And before that, it was Covid, and our father died from it..." he trails off.

"Oh, I'm so sorry," says Isabella. He has known loss. He can empathize about the ache of grief. And he is evidently close to his sister, as she and Julian had been. "So much sadness," she says, rubbing her thumb against his upper arm.

"Now I am worried for my sister," he says. "It is big mess. When she must leave our country, we are texting all the time, but," he snaps his fingers, "like *this* suddenly nothing, and she does not answer calls or texts. I do not know what has happened. I am thinking it is not possible to lose somebody today with cell phones and Internet, but I cannot find her."

Isabella swivels in her seat to look at him, though she can only just make out his outline in the darkened auditorium. "This is terrible! Have you tried your embassy?"

"I tried there, I tried immigration places, I keep asking here at Peabody. I went to where she is living, and the person there said perhaps Orson can tell me where she is."

He turns back to the stage, and Isabella follows his look.

"Oh!" she says. "We've missed your chance to talk to him."

Orson is seated at the keyboard again, and he plays a chord so that the singers can pick out their pitches.

"It's okay," Sevastyan whispers. "I can wait."

Isabella subsides back into her seat. She shifts her body to lean her upper arm against his, trying to communicate to him her empathy. She's is astounded that he hasn't spoken about any of this before. It's no wonder he's been distant and offhand—he's had it on his mind all the time.

The new piece that Orson and the singers are working on is the scene when the self-important Malvolio scolds Sir Toby, Sir Andrew, and Feste the Fool for their noisy late-night revel, and they decide to retaliate with Maria's help. Isabella is quite taken aback by Drew Lilley's comedic timing as Sir Andrew Aguecheek. She's heard his recordings before, but she has found him so anemic in person that his flair for comedy is the last thing she would have expected.

The music, with its Malvolio leitmotif, stops and starts with off beats and syncopation, and it comes across as a hilarious romp—completely different from the yearning Olivia aria, or the intricate harmonic play of the quartet, and yet still with a homogeneity of sound that has Orson's handwriting on it. Isabella is surprised by the hilarity. In her experience of him, Orson has always taken himself so seriously, and yet this music is shot through with a wonderful sense of humor.

Despite the levity of the scene—or perhaps because of it—Orson is even more of a perfectionist, stopping the singers repeatedly to point out rhythmic inaccuracies and to correct intonation, pulling the ensemble tightly together. After their first "stagger-through," as he calls it, he shades his eyes once again and peers out into the darkened auditorium.

"Any thoughts, Isabella?"

"No, it's sounding really good for a first run-through. It's hilarious."

"Okay," he says, turning back to the singers. "Let's play it through once without stopping, and then that will be it for today."

Isabella watches Orson conducting from the harpsichord. She's struck once again by how extraordinarily gifted he is, with a phenomenal natural talent as a keyboard player, and now this relatively newfound talent for composition. She loves his music and his musicality, and, not for the first time, she wonders why she could never transfer that love to him as a person. It's a part of who he is, after all, and it was pretty obvious how he felt about her throughout the whole *Venus Hottentot* project. She *should* have been in love with him. She'd even half-heartedly tried to talk herself into it, but she couldn't manufacture something that wasn't there—any more than she's been able to snuff out these feelings for Sevastyan.

She knows that her reluctance to sing in Orson's new opera isn't only because she's been distraught about losing Julian. The opera promises to be extraordinary. But she's wary of placing herself in the same stressful situation that she'd found herself in during *The Venus Hottentot,* of trying to be open and trusting towards Orson musically, while at the same time needing to keep him at arm's length emotionally. In her experience, it can be just as unsettling to be on the receiving end of unrequited feelings as it's painful to be on the one-sided end. Isabella is so lost in her thoughts that it is only when the music stops that she pulls herself back into the present moment, sitting here in the dark auditorium, her arm resting against Sevastyan's, feeling his warm, open presence next to her.

"Isabella? Can we go somewhere to talk?" calls Orson. "I only have the hall booked for another few minutes."

"Let's meet back at my apartment," she says.

"Ah! A party at *la bella* Isabella's!" crows Tobia.

"We'll do that another time, Tobia," she says.

"I just have a few notes for the singers, and then I'll meet you there," says Orson.

"Fine."

He turns back to confer with the singers.

Sevastyan shifts forward to the edge of his seat, preparing to stand. "I will quickly try to talk to him before he leaves," he says.

Isabella looks at his profile, wishing she could hold on to this newly accessible version of him. She doesn't want to risk letting the tenuous connection slip away and finding out later that he has become cool and distant again.

"I hope I'll have the opportunity to meet your sister soon," she says softly.

"I hope this too," he says, turning to her and speaking low in return. "She is also musician, so you will have much to talk about with her."

"I wish you could have met my brother, Julian," says Isabella. "In some ways you remind me a little bit of him. He was also reserved, but there was so much warmth and empathy deep down and, in his way, he was very gifted."

Sevastyan shakes his head. "You are giving me too much praise," he says.

Isabella becomes aware that the auditorium is completely silent except for their murmuring voices. She looks towards the stage. It is empty. They are the only ones still here.

Sevastyan stands quickly. "Oh no!" He puts his palms on either side of his head. "I am too late. I have missed him."

"It's my fault," says Isabella, standing too. "I'm sorry, I shouldn't have kept you talking."

"прокляття!" he exclaims.

Isabella assumes this is a Ukrainian curse. He is clearly upset.

"Listen," she says, "my apartment isn't far, so you can come back with me and speak to him there."

"But I must go now with message for my friend."

"Where?"

He gives her the name of the coffee shop where António works.

"That's just around the corner from here."

"Yes."

"Well, you go and give him your message, and then we can leave."

"I do not know if he will be there at this time. It may be that I will have to wait, and I do not know for how long."

Isabella reaches down into her bag and, after a quick rummage, gives him her business card.

"Here's my card," she says. "If your friend isn't there, leave my card with a message for him to come there, and you come on there yourself. It's within walking distance."

Sevastyan hesitates. "Are you sure?" he asks.

"Quite sure."

"But you do not even know my friend."

"If he's your friend, then I'm sure."

His face lights up in what is clearly a smile behind his mask, and it acts on her like a magnet. With no conscious thought or volition, she reaches her arm around his neck in a quick, fervent embrace. She pulls back and she can just make out his extraordinary eyes in the darkness. They are crinkled at the corners with a look that she can't read—something surprised, something amused, something quizzical. Whatever it is, it's a welcome change from the indifference of before.

SEVASTYAN

SEVASTYAN RETURNS HER LOOK, trying to gauge the astonishing—but certainly not unwelcome—embrace from this woman, this Isabella. Their eyes, he finds, are on the same level. She is tall for a woman, like Vira. She is the one to break their gaze. She picks up the leather bag at her feet and pulls it over her shoulder, her movement releasing a waft of woody perfume.

"I'll wait for you here," she says.

"No, please do not wait," he says, "because then maybe you will not be in time at your apartment." He looks down at her card, then tucks it into his pocket. "I have your address, and I will come after I finish with my friend."

"I'd better get going, then, or Orson will get there before me. He has a habit of being early for everything," she laughs. "I promise I won't let him get away this time."

Sevastyan smiles in response. His agitation about Vira is not diminished in any way, but it is now existing side by side with the pull of this intriguing woman. He knows that he should also be making a move to go, and he tries to think of some parting words that won't break the fragile connection there seems to be between them. He is intrigued and baffled. The logical, mathematical part of his mind tells him that there is obviously some mix-up. But her magnetism makes him wish with all his heart that there isn't. They are standing very close, and he longs to close the small space between them to lean forward and embrace her again. The auditorium lights slam on, and they both jump, then laugh.

She looks into his eyes. "See you soon?"

"Yes," he says.

He watches her walk down the aisle to an exit near the stage. Once she has gone, he turns and leaves the way he came.

ORSON

ORSON STRIDES UP TO THE DOUBLE BRASS DOORS of Isabella's apartment building and vigorously yanks the right one open. He's still as keyed up as a vibrating piano string from the rehearsal. And he's confident that if Isabella has suggested meeting at her place, she must have come around to the idea of singing the role of Olivia.

"Dr. Carradine!" says Fausto. "It's been too long."

"Hi, Fausto. You're looking well."

"I'm looking fat, you mean," Fausto laughs. "Ah well, we all get older. Except for you—you look the same as the first day I met you."

"You mean I'm looking just as much of a mess as ever," Orson banters back. "How's the family?"

"Good, good. My wife still has her deli, and our daughter helps out there now."

"I must visit again. Nobody makes better pesto than Nellie!"

"She will love to see you."

"Is Isabella here?" asks Orson.

"No, she hasn't come back yet. There's someone else waiting to see her." He jerks his thumb behind him with what seems to be a long-suffering look.

Orson looks further into the lobby. Sevastyan is sitting in one of the chairs in front of a huge ornate mirror by a potted palm, his slim frame hunched and tense, a lock of his dark hair falling across his forehead, those green eyes meeting his. Orson's pulse lurches.

"What are you doing here?" His voice is sharper, louder, than he intended. He is suddenly breathless as he stares across the lobby. *What on earth is there about the familiar sight of Sevastyan to disconcert you?* he berates himself.

Sevastyan says, "Isabella gave me music scores, and I must bring them back now."

Orson walks across the lobby and looks down at the slim figure sitting there. After hesitating for a second, Orson sits in the other chair. It must be seeing Sevastyan out of context that has given him a jolt. They have been in close proximity before, when they've made music together and when they went to the exhibition at the mansion, and they've shared some fairly intimate moments. He doesn't understand why he suddenly feels off kilter, and it's not a feeling he likes. It reminds him too much of how edgy he'd felt around Isabella during *The Venus Hottentot*.

He glances sideways at Sevastyan, who looks so vulnerable that suddenly Orson wants nothing more than to—what, protect him? It's absurd. He hasn't felt this unsettled by anyone since those early days of Isabella, when her talent and her beauty had so overwhelmed him. Why on earth does he keep thinking of Isabella and his infatuation with her? He's not infatuated with Sevastyan! He *likes* him, sure enough, and he's mesmerized by his musicality, but he's never thought anything more about him than a mild curiosity as to how he came by his extraordinary musical knowledge. He's never thought of *any* guy, androgynous or not, in that particular way. He doesn't even like most men; they're generally too competitive and in-your-face. So, what is it about Sevastyan—now, at this moment—that makes him feel as if his bowels are doing some kind of convoluted, contorted gymnastics?

"How was the run-through?" asks Sevastyan.

"Good. It went really well," says Orson, thankfully grabbing onto a line of conversation. "I've heard the quartet in my head, of course, but it was great to hear it with their voices."

"And that part where all four voices come in together for the first time?"

"Perfect! I may need to rework some phrases in the final coda, but overall I'm really pleased with the way it hangs together."

"What did Isabella think?"

"She asked me to come back here to talk about it, so I'm pretty sure she's going to agree to do it."

"I am so glad."

"Thanks again, so much, for persevering with her."

Sevastyan smiles. "It wasn't me. It is all your music—"

"Shall I call up to Mía and ask if she will let you into the apartment?" calls Fausto.

"Uh … sure!" says Orson. Maybe a change of scene will make him feel less on edge.

While Fausto makes the call, the two of them sit in their separate chairs in a hiatus of awkwardness. Orson has always found it easy to talk to Sevastyan—about music, viols, some shared interest, or even some intimacy—but he feels inexplicably on edge with him now, and he doesn't want to come up with another topic of conversation only to have it interrupted again by Fausto. He looks down at Sevastyan's long hands resting on the music scores across his thighs. The wrist bone protrudes from his left cuff, and Orson has a vivid mental image of watching Sevastyan reaching for the scattered music pages when he'd come to clean his music room that first time. Orson had thought then, too, that Sevastyan's hands were too slender and smooth for the rough work of cleaning.

"She says you can go up," says Fausto.

"Good." Orson almost jumps up. He looks down at Sevastyan. "Are you coming?"

Sevastyan shoots a glance at Fausto, and Orson follows his look. Fausto grins and jerks his head towards the elevator.

Sevastyan picks up his viol at his feet, slips his backpack over one shoulder, and follows Orson to the bank of elevators. Orson pokes at the button, and another awkward silence ensues as they wait for the elevator doors to open. Sevastyan presses himself into a corner, holding the music scores tightly across his chest. "Fausto doesn't like me," he says, "because I pushed myself in when I came to see Isabella the first time."

Orson grins. "It's hard to imagine you being pushy."

Sevastyan just stares down at the floor of the elevator, not saying anything.

"Are you okay?" Orson asks. He's been so preoccupied with his own feelings of dislocation around Sevastyan that it hasn't dawned on him until now how nervy Sevastyan is. When Sevastyan just shrugs without answering, Orson says, "What's going on?"

The green eyes flick up to meet his for a split second, but look down again. "I'm—" he stops himself. "It's nothing."

But clearly, it is something. Orson studies Sevastyan's bowed head. He longs to pull this beautiful, slender, troubled person against his body and is on the point of yielding to the urge when the elevator pings and the doors open.

VIRA

VIRA TRAILS BEHIND ORSON into Isabella's apartment to the enthusiastic accompaniment of Mía's voice.

"I'm so excited to see you, Orson! I've missed you."

"You're looking very well, Mía."

"Oh, I'm fine. Come and wait in the living room. Isabella texted me to offer you a drink while you wait."

"I'll have a glass of red wine, thanks. What about you, Sevastyan?"

"Just some water, please."

"Oh, come on! We're celebrating," Orson says.

"Really, just some water, thank you."

The last thing Vira feels is a sense of celebration. She is too caught up in the cross currents of every-which-way feelings. She had never expected to meet up with Orson here, and when she saw him stride into the lobby downstairs, she'd felt the blood drain from her face so quickly that if she hadn't been sitting down, she might have keeled over. Standing in the living room now, she knows that she could simply leave the scores for Isabella and go, but she wants to stay, just to be with him a little longer.

When Mía withdraws her bright personality to go and see to the drinks, an awkward silence falls between them again. Orson is full of nervous energy, even more than usual, no doubt because he's keyed up to hear Isabella's response to the run-through this afternoon. Vira has become used to Orson's volatility—edgy, enthusiastic, tense, even tetchy at times—but now he seems awkward, unsure, almost shy, which is completely out of character for him. It's something to do with Isabella, obviously.

Orson wanders over to study the collection of CDs, and Vira walks to the windows at the end of the room. She props her viol in the corner, drops her backpack on the floor next to it, and sits down with her back to the window, holding the Dowland scores on her lap.

Orson glances at her, then turns away from the CDs and flops himself down on the chaise longue where Isabella was sitting when Vira came to see her the first time. He picks up a magazine from a neatly arranged stack on the side table. "So, Isabella still subscribes to *Gramophone*," he says. "She can't be that much off the grid then."

Vira sits still, watching his bony fingers as they flip through the pages of the magazine.

"Hey!" he says. "There's a new recording of the Bach cello suites played on bass viol—that would be a good marketing angle for our production."

Our production, she thinks. Could it be that he is thinking of including her in it? Surely not. She must have misunderstood. She mustn't mistake fantasy for reality. She's suddenly hot with the late afternoon sun on her back, and she slips her jacket off, letting it fall behind her onto the seat of the chair. Orson looks up from the *Gramophone*, watching her movements, then he goes back to his paging.

The clink-clink of glasses precedes Mía coming into the room with a tray of drinks. As she places the tray on a side table, Vira hears a key in the front door.

"Ah!" says Mía, "here is Isabella."

Vira looks at the glinting glasses: her water in a crystal tumbler, the movement of Orson's red wine making a dancing dot of reflected color on the silver tray, and a champagne flute with condensation on the outside mirroring the rising bubbles inside. She knows that the minutes of her time here are evaporating, like the bubbles. She will hand over the scores to Isabella, she may take a sip or two of water, and then there will be no excuse for her not to leave. She is achingly aware that the little star-struck episode of her life involving Orson and Isabella is coming to an end.

ISABELLA

AS ISABELLA WALKS INTO THE SUNNY LIVING ROOM, Orson pulls his rangy height from the chaise longue and tosses a copy of *Gramophone* magazine on top of the pile on the table. This is one of the things that has always irritated her about him—his lack of tidiness and order.

"Isabella!" He says warmly, walking towards her and stooping to kiss her cheek.

Over his shoulder, Isabella sees Sevastyan stand up from the chair by the window, silhouetted against the light, his face in shadow.

"How did you get here so quickly?" she exclaims.

"Um … I used the city circulator bus as usual."

"You've changed your clothes…"

"I was hot. I've just taken off my jacket."

He seems guarded again. Is it because Orson is here? Or

because they are meeting in her apartment, where there has been tension between them before? Has he had time to mull over her quick embrace and think better of it?

"Sevastyan—" she reaches her hand towards him.

"I have brought your Dowland scores to give back to you," he says quickly, speaking over her.

"No, keep them!" She glances at Orson, at the eager, expectant look on his face. She takes a breath, steeling herself. What she has to say to him won't get any easier, and she needs to get this over with now. "Your music is gorgeous, Orson. You've really extended yourself. It's inventive, and new, and exciting..."

"I sense a 'but,'" he says.

"I'm not ready yet."

"Isabella—"

"Please, Orson, don't try to talk me into it. I wanted to tell you to your face—I just can't take on a full production at this time. If I'm going to get back into singing, I need to start small." She glances at Sevastyan, still standing against the light. "Sevastyan and I have talked about working on a recital of Elizabethan songs—"

"Sevastyan?" Orson also looks over to Sevastyan, his question wary, almost accusatory.

"No!" says Sevastyan, "I've brought the music back."

Isabella jumps in quickly, not wanting to hear Sevastyan's refusal, keeping her eyes fixed on Orson. "When we played through your aria, we worked so well together. It gave me confidence that I might be able to get back to singing again. I need to build on that slowly."

Orson hasn't taken his eyes off Sevastyan. "What have you been up to, Sevastyan?"

"He hasn't 'been up to' anything, Orson," Isabella says.

Orson ignores her, still staring at Sevastyan. "You were

supposed to be my emissary to persuade Isabella to sing Olivia for me. Meanwhile, you've been secretly hatching this plan. Now I understand why you kept trying to tell me not to push her to do it. You wanted to keep her for yourself."

"No—" Sevastyan protests.

"Orson, no!" Isabella speaks over Sevastyan. "He pleaded your case insistently—annoyingly so. I'm just not ready to take this on. It's as simple as that."

Orson is still staring at Sevastyan, as if she hadn't spoken. "I put my trust in you," he says, "and all this time, you've been going behind my back, deceiving me."

"I have *not* been deceiving you," says Sevastyan, his voice low but urgent. "Not about this."

"Oh, no?" says Orson sharply. "About what, then?"

Isabella jumps in again. "He knows how I feel about him." She looks at Sevastyan, willing him to be as he was this afternoon. "And today you made me think you felt the same."

"Today?" says Sevastyan. "But—"

"Why do you deny it?" she says, staring at him, her throat tightening. He confided his anxieties about his sister to her. He'd not rebuffed her when she put her hand on his arm. He responded when she embraced him. She hadn't imagined any of that.

"Who's lying here?" says Orson. "If it's you, Sevastyan, then you can leave here right now, and I never want to see you again. How could I ever trust you again if you've been playing some double game?"

Into this zinging tension, comes the modulated baritone of Malvon. "Excuse me," he says.

MALVON

IT IS FIVE O'CLOCK, and Malvon has been patiently waiting all day to speak to Isabella. When he arrived at nine o'clock sharp as usual this morning, his second yellow bow tie perfectly knotted and matching the triangle of handkerchief protruding from his breast pocket, she had still been in her room. He knows her routine: she rises late, and then goes into the kitchen to make coffee in the Bialetti percolator on the stovetop. At some point in the morning, she will come into the music room to talk to him about the day's business. It is the high point of his day. It's true that with her having taken a break from her singing career he's been finding it more and more difficult to find any business to do for her, but today he'd decided to go through her emails and organize them into folders, and he'd planned to use a discussion about the naming of the various folders to lead into the conversation about the email she had sent him.

When, at last, she had come in to speak with him late this

morning—much later than usual in fact—it had only been to say that she was going out to listen to a rehearsal, that she would be back in the late afternoon, and that he shouldn't feel obliged to wait around. But he *had* to see her. He can't possibly wait through the whole weekend before speaking with her about her email.

He'd heard Orson and Sevastyan come into the apartment half an hour ago, and quietly got up from the desk to go and close the pocket door to the music room so that he and Isabella would have privacy when she came in to talk to him, as he was certain she would. When he heard her voice in the entrance hall, he'd perked himself up, made quite sure his tie was straight, and fixed his eyes on the door. But she had gone directly into the living room. He'd stood up and put his ear to the door to gauge what was going on out there, and he heard the rise and fall of increasingly agitated voices.

He watched the minute hand on his wristwatch as it counted down the seconds to five o'clock. He would give it until then, he decided, and then he would take matters into his own hands. He put on his jacket, placed his packed briefcase on the chair, opened the door of the music room, and stepped into the living room.

"Excuse me," he repeats, this time more loudly, since nobody paid any attention to him the first time.

Isabella turns to him, her lovely eyes wide and glistening. After a moment she says, "What is it, Malvon?"

"I need to speak to you."

"This is not a good time."

"It is important," he says. He reaches his hand into his inside breast pocket where he keeps her printed email next to his heart, and takes it out. "I need to speak with you about this."

Before he can stop her, Isabella reaches out and takes the email from his hand, just as the front doorbell rings. There's a moment of suspended animation in the living room, then Mía ushers in a young Latino.

"This is António," says Mía. She confers with him quickly in Spanish. "He says Sevastyan left your card for him, Isabella, and told him to come to your apartment."

Everyone in the room turns their attention to where Sevastyan is standing silhouetted against the window.

Sevastyan says, "I—"

This is all getting out of hand. Malvon is determined to focus Isabella's attention on him and their issue.

"Isabella!" He projects his voice over the restiveness in the room. "We really must speak."

She glances back at him, and then down at the paper in her hand, as if only just remembering that it is there. She unfolds it and her eyes run down the page.

"No!" says Malvon. "Not here."

"What's this, Malvon?"

"We must talk *privately*."

Malvon wants to snatch the email back from her. It was not supposed to be like this, skimmed in a hurry in a room full of people. He wanted to dwell on it with her, pore over every word, and respond accordingly.

She looks up at him. "What is this?" she asks again.

He feels just the faintest trace of indignation that she would even ask. "It's your email," he says.

"It's not mine."

"Of *course* it is." Why is she claiming that it isn't her email? He drops his voice to a fierce whisper. "We *must* talk privately."

"There's nothing to talk about, Malvon, this isn't anything to do with me."

"But it's from your own email account—I've just filed it in a folder in your sent box!"

"Well, that may be so, but I didn't send it."

Malvon stares at the page that Isabella is still holding and the words swim in front of his eyes like little tadpoles skittering across a pond.

"You're the only one aside from me who has access to my emails," says Isabella. Then she looks across to where Mía is standing by the door behind him. After an aching pause during which Malvon feels his throat tighten as if he might—God forbid—cry, Isabella says, "Mía?"

And then Malvon hears a babbling torrent from Mía. "It was meant to be a joke. He was so mean to me, and I wanted to teach him a lesson. He told me I was a foreigner and I didn't belong here. Then ICE came to my apartment in the middle of the night, demanding to see my papers, and I'm sure he had something to do with that. I was upset and angry, and I wanted to make a fool of him."

When Mía eventually stops talking, there is a chill of silence in the room. With infinite care, Malvon reaches out to pull the page from between Isabella's fingers. He looks down at the toes of his highly polished shoes and sees them turn towards the interleading door of the music room. He watches first one foot and then the other step across the pile of the carpet. In the music room, he opens his briefcase and slips the page into the front compartment. He latches the case again, picks it up, and walks through the living room towards the front door.

"Mía!" he hears Isabella's voice from behind him. "Go after him! Make it right! I expect you to make it right."

Malvon steps through the front door and meticulously pulls it shut behind him. There's an elevator on the floor. He gets onto it quickly and presses his finger to door close button, hearing the apartment door open just before the elevator clanks shut.

SEVASTYAN

SEVASTYAN DOUBLE-CHECKS THE NUMBER 501 of the apartment building, and pushes open the heavy brass door.

"You again!" exclaims the concierge at the front desk. "How come you're always arriving and never leaving?"

Sevastyan is taken aback by the greeting—is it a greeting?—wondering if this is some American idiomatic familiarity that he has yet to learn. He resorts to the response he always defaults to when in doubt, and grins widely.

"Well, go on up!" says the concierge.

"Thanks," says Sevastyan.

He leans into the corner of the elevator cab; all the walking is taking a toll on his back. When he steps out on the top floor, he finds that the door is open. He taps gently. No response. Through the open door he can see Isabella standing in a room across the entrance hall. He crosses the hall to stand in the doorway.

"I am sorry," he says, looking directly at Isabella. "The door was open, so I just came in. Sorry I am late."

She stares at him without speaking, her eyes wide, her face frozen. A figure at the other end of the room steps forward from the window with an inarticulate cry.

"Vironka!"

Vira runs to him, her arms around his neck, her face burrowed into his shoulder, and he wraps his arms around her, crushing her in a close hug, relief surging through his veins with a fizz.

"Sobka ... Sobka..." Her breath is warm against him.

"At *last!*" he says in Ukrainian.

"I've been frantic," she says. "It's been so frightening."

"What's been going on? I kept getting a message that your number wasn't operating, then I got a complete stranger on your new number. Fariba Mehta says you had a bad experience."

"Oh, Sobka, I've got so much to tell you."

"Wait." He draws back a little from their embrace as he remembers where they are. "Speak in English," he says, switching himself, "so that everyone can understand."

She nods, and turns back towards the room, keeping a tight grip on him.

"The same face," says Orson, standing just behind Isabella and staring at Sevastyan, "the same unmistakable eyes, almost the same voice and height. It's like some kind of optical illusion."

"Is it you, Sevastyan?" asks António.

"António!" says Sevastyan. "You made it."

"How have you divided yourself?" António looks from him to Vira, and back again.

Sevastyan turns to Isabella, and makes the introduction. "This is my sister, Vira," he says.

Isabella expels her breath sharply, as if someone has just thumped her on the back.

"*Sister!*" The word explodes from Orson.

For a moment, nobody speaks or moves.

Isabella gives a shaky laugh. "I need to sit," she says, plumping herself down on the chair nearest her.

Vira pulls Sevastyan to sit with her on a love seat opposite Isabella.

"Take off your mask," she murmurs in Ukrainian. He stuffs it into a pocket.

António sits on a chair near the door. Orson returns to the chaise longue.

In the expectant silence, Vira closes her eyes for a moment and takes a deep breath. Then she says, "Yes, I am Vira." She shoots a look across the room to Orson then looks away, but he continues to stare at her as if he's trying to bore right into her soul with his eyes. "And this is my beloved twin brother, Sevastyan." Vira reaches for Sevastyan's hand, and holds it tightly between both of her own. "In 2020, we made plans to come to America. I wished to find studentship—"

"Scholarship," Sevastyan substitutes.

"Scholarship in performance practice for viol, and for Sevastyan—" she breaks off and asks him in Ukrainian, "what is the term in English?"

"Research assistant in quantum computing," he says, picking up the story, falling into their rhythm of completing each other's thoughts and sentences as they have always done. "I went to consulate to ask for student visas," says Sevastyan, "but we did not know if we could come."

"It was first pandemic and then war," says Vira.

"And they said women and children and old people must leave, so Vira took train from Lviv to Poland, but I must stay behind with other men."

In the riveted attention fixed on them, Sevastyan has been caught up with trying to explain how they got here, but now they've reached the point where it all fell apart. His anxiety ratchets up again, and he turns to Vira. "But what happened? Why did you stop texting?" he asks.

"I..." She stops and looks down at their clasped hands, and then up into Sevastyan's face. She blurts out, "I was attacked."

Sevastyan feels punched in the chest. Has he heard her correctly? He stares at her as everyone in the room overlaps with a jumble of exclamations and questions. Vira holds his gaze, then she turns her head and studies the carpet at her feet. She waits, breathing deeply.

She repeats, "I was attacked," and she goes on in a rush, "by this man. I got away, but I lost everything—my cell phone, my papers." She looks into Sevastyan's face, her eyes glistening. "It was..." she can't think of the English word, and says, "жахливий."

"Terrifying," Sevastyan translates.

"I did not know what I can do to be safe until you came," she goes on. "I missed you. I longed for you to be with me, and I wanted to be like you—sure and full of sense. So, I thought I would try to *be* you, to pretend to be you, to protect myself until you came."

"О, мій любий!" Sevastyan wraps his arms around her, pulling her head onto his shoulder.

MÍA

IT TAKES WHAT FEELS LIKE AN AGE for another elevator to come. When it eventually deposits her on the first floor, Mía sprints across the lobby and bursts out into the late afternoon sunlight. Malvon is across the street, in the process of unlocking the door of his beige Buick.

"Malvon!" she calls.

His head jerks, so she knows he's heard her, but he makes as if he hasn't.

"Malvon!" she shouts again. "Wait! Please wait!"

She runs across the road, dodging in front of a car. The driver honks and bellows at her out the open window. She gets to Malvon's car just as he's managed to unlock the car, slide into the driver's seat, and slam the door. He locks it. She bangs with her palms on the window of the driver's side.

"Open up, Malvon! I must talk to you. Please, open up."

He puts the key into the ignition. The engine turns over.

Mía abandons her post at the driver's window, and runs to stand in front of the car. Malvon looks stonily ahead, keeping the engine running. They are locked in this impasse for a full minute. He turns off the engine. She comes around to the driver's window again.

"Malvon," she calls through the window. "I'm sorry, okay? I'm sorry!"

He continues staring straight ahead. He is *so* infuriating. Mía wants nothing more than to turn her back on him and never see him again in her life. She knows—as much as she can know without *actually* knowing—that Malvon called ICE on her. For that alone she wishes could punch him. But Isabella, beloved Isabella, expects her to make this right. She will just have to force herself to eat a huge slice of humble pie, even if it does give her emotional indigestion.

"Malvon, look, I know what I did was bad. You can be as mad at me as you like. But it's not Isabella's fault. You can't take it out on her." He sits like a stone, as if he can't hear her, although a passing cyclist looks back at her with a quizzical expression because she is shouting so loudly at Malvon through the window. "Please," she goes on, "will you come in on Monday as usual, so we can talk about it, the three of us together?" She considers saying that Isabella will never forgive her if she doesn't make it right, but it occurs to her just in time that this would be the perfect incentive for Malvon not to do so.

"Please, Malvon, I'm really, *really* sorry. Please say you'll come back on Monday so we can try to smooth things over with Isabella."

He turns to her finally, and surveys her through the car window. "I will come," he says, his voice muffled behind the glass, "but only to speak with Miss Foiani. I will never forgive you, and I never want to see you ever again."

"Fine!" says Mía, "I'll tell her."

Malvon swivels his head away from her and turns the key in the ignition again. Mía steps away from the Buick as he puts the car into gear, and eases away from the curb. She stands in his empty parking space looking after him until he turns the corner, then she crosses the road and walks quickly towards the apartment building. A bubble of elation rises in her at the thought that she won't ever have anything to do with him again. But she still has to face a reckoning with Isabella.

ORSON

ORSON'S EYES ARE RIVETED on the slim figure on the other side of the room. Sevastyan a *woman*? He studies the lithe grace, the long fingers, the bony wrists. He envisions again how she'd reached for the scattered pages of his music, her wrist extending from the sleeve of her shirt, her hands too slender and smooth for the rough work of being a cleaner. He's always thought that the Sevastyan he knows was a bit androgynous—but a *woman*?

He studies her body. She is thin, like her brother, broad-shouldered, long limbed. There's no outline of breasts that he can detect under her loose-fitting T-shirt. Her green eyes catch on Orson's—as before, when she'd said, *Yes, I am Vira*—and then they slip away again. The impulse to cross the room to her, to pull her up from the love seat and into his arms, is close to overwhelming.

"Were you hurt?" Sevastyan asks.

"Cuts and bruises," Vira says. "Not so bad."

Sevastyan reaches to touch her. "Your hair," he says.

She smiles at him with the deep warmth and affection of all the years. "We are the same again, like when we were little."

As Orson sits there watching her, things start clicking into place one by one—as if he's playing through a difficult passage at half tempo, first with the right hand, then with the left, and gradually piecing it all back together again. He understands, now, Vira's edgy reticence, her vague androgyny, the air of something enigmatic about her that he could never quite fathom.

Something else clicks into place. When he thought Vira, as Sevastyan, had been deceiving him by making secret plans with Isabella, the sick disappointment he felt was about more than just a sense of betrayal; it was tinged with jealousy—and not about *Isabella*, as it would have been as little as a month ago, but about Vira. Now, as he accepts Vira's protestation that she hadn't deceived him—not about *this*—he empathizes with Isabella's bewilderment. The disconcerting desire he'd felt downstairs in the lobby and in the elevator makes perfect sense in this drastically new light. He knows that Curtis is pansexual, drawn to the particular qualities of a *person* regardless of their sex or gender identity, and Orson has been on the point of believing that he has a similar orientation. Because there is, quite suddenly, no shred of a doubt that he is deeply, compellingly attracted to this gifted, beautiful, appealing person he has been thinking of all along as Sevastyan.

ISABELLA

ISABELLA STARES ACROSS THE ROOM at Sevastyan and Vira sitting side by side on the love seat. She feels as if she's been trying to listen to two completely disparate pieces of music at the same time. The person she's thought herself falling in love with is a woman, and the man she had such a strong pull towards this afternoon is a stranger.

It's unnerving how alike the two of them are—not only their distinctive eyes, but also the exact way that their hair falls over their foreheads, their slight frames, their gestures, their speech inflections. She can't take her eyes off them.

A distraction comes in the form of Mía, who appears at the doorway looking subdued. She looks at Isabella, her plea written clearly all over her face.

"Did you talk to him?" Isabella asks.

"Yes."

"And?"

"He will never forgive me," Mia says. "You know him. Malvon is not someone who forgives. But he says he will come on Monday—to iron things out with you, but only *you*."

"Well, we can decide on the best way forward then." Isabella is not at all sure that she either wants or needs Malvon to keep looking after her business affairs, but she hopes she'll be able to smooth his ruffled feathers at least.

"I'm sorry." Mía stares at a spot on the rug just in front of Isabella's chair, her voice is so low it's almost inaudible. "It was a stupid thing to do."

"Yes."

"He just makes me *so* mad."

"He has a way of doing that," says Isabella drily.

Mía's eyes meet at Isabella's with a glimmer of their usual spark.

In the scheme of things, with two Sevastyans now in the room, Mía's transgression is less of an issue than it might otherwise have been. Isabella decides to move on. "Well, why don't you go and organize some drinks for everyone now," she says. "I think we could all do with one."

"Of course!" Mía jumps at the idea.

"*¿Puedo ayudarte?*" António asks Mía.

"*Sí por favor,*" she says.

As António stands to go and help Mía, Sevastyan says, "António, I have something for you." He crosses to him, pulling an envelope from the pocket of his jacket. "After I left the message for you at the coffee shop, I got a text from the Refugee and Immigrant Center, and I went down to fetch this." António takes the envelope. "These are forms from pro bono lawyers who work with the center. Fariba Mehta says you can contact them, and see if one will take your case. It will take time, she says, and it will be difficult, but it is not impossible."

António takes the envelope and slides his forefinger under the flap to tear it open.

Sevastyan looks across at Isabella. "This is what made me so late. I am sorry."

"It doesn't matter now," says Isabella. His lateness is the least of it. How on earth can she begin to untangle the ramifications of these two Sevastyans?

António looks up from the forms in his hand, his face alight. "Thank you, Sevastyan! This is so great." Then he looks past Sevastyan at Vira. "I thought you were him on Wednesday," he says.

"I only understood after," she says. "I went back to find you, but you were already gone."

António looks from one to the other. "You are like two halves of one apple," he says. The room relaxes into laughter, and António turns to follow Mía to the kitchen.

Isabella takes a speck of comfort from António's exchange with Vira. At least she's not the only one who has mistaken one twin for the other. But she still feels disconcerted and embarrassed, and she knows that it is up to her to clear up the misunderstanding. She would so much prefer not to try to do so in front of an audience, and she says to Sevastyan, "I love the light in the music room at this time of day. Let me show you."

He looks across at Vira, and she returns his gaze, clear-eyed. It's as if some unspoken, unseen communication has passed between them. He turns back to Isabella and says, "Sure."

The late afternoon sun is lying in long, amber blocks across the kilim rug in the music room, and the light has a warm, honeyed glow.

Sevastyan stops on the threshold. "Oh!" he says. "I see. It is a beautiful room."

"It's my favorite," she says.

His eyes travel around the room, taking in the piano, the music scores, "You are pianist?"

"A singer. Or, I was. I haven't been singing lately."

He advances into the room and stops a little in front of her. "Why?" he asks.

How can she explain the overwhelming sorrow she has felt for the past six months? "I've been unhappy," she says simply. "My brother died recently."

"I am so sorry to hear this," Sevastyan says, his voice almost inaudible, his body leaning into her infinitesimally. He glances towards the wall that divides the music room from the sitting room where they have just left Vira. "I cannot think how terrible that must be for you. These ten days ... not to hear from Vira..." He leaves the thought unspoken.

The pause feels weighted, a little jagged, and Isabella searches for an opening into the conversation she knows she needs to have. She crosses the room to sit on the upholstered bench where Vira had unpacked her viol. After a moment, Sevastyan follows her and sits down next to her. Vira, as Sevastyan, would never have done that, Isabella thinks. He angles his body towards her and that small movement gives her the small propulsion of confidence she needs.

"This afternoon..." she begins, looking away from him and out of the long windows at the fading day. But she will have to go further back than this afternoon, she realizes, to explain it. "You see," she goes on, "Orson sent Vira, this person who said his name ... her name ... was Sevastyan, to try to talk me into singing in the new opera that Orson is working on—the one you heard at the run-through today." She glances at him, and he nods. "And he—or she—came, and we played through some of Orson's music together." She hesitates, trying to find the best way to pull her thoughts together to articulate the experience. "There was something about the way we made music together, the instinctive synergy we shared about tempo and dynamics and phrasing ... it unlocked something inside me." She pauses again. He waits, quietly attentive. "For the first time in months I was feeling something that wasn't the black despair I'd felt ever since Julian died. I was so grateful, so relieved. And it made me think that I had a deep emotional connection to him ... to her ... to..." She stops, willing him to understand.

After a moment, he says, "And this afternoon, you thought that I was this person."

She nods. "It was a combination of everything all jumbled together. Listening to Orson's music stirred up the feelings I'd had when I made music with that other Sevastyan. I couldn't see you properly in the dark, I could only really sense you. And you were warm and open towards me, where the other Sevastyan has always been so distant." The light in the room is shifting from amber to a cooler blue. "But even though the Sevastyan I knew wouldn't allow me to get close to him, there was something—something more, even, than the way he made music—that took away my sadness. He seemed to draw me in. I can't explain it."

"I know what you mean. She has that gift. She does it also for me, and I have watched her do it with other people. She has something inside. It is like a quiet place of calm, and you want to reach in and touch it."

"Yes!" That so exactly describes what it had been like. She looks at him directly for the first time since they have come into the room. Seeing him in the late afternoon light, without his face-mask, she registers the jawline, the shadow of stubble, that define him as male. Is he enough like Vira on the inside that the feelings she had for Sevastyan this afternoon could have been for him, and not only a mistaken transfer?

"How alike are you and your sister?" Then she laughs, catching herself. "Well, obviously, you are exceptionally alike in looks. But are you alike in your personalities as well?"

He considers this for a moment. Then he says, "It is more like two halves of one person." He grins. "Two halves of one apple, the way António said. Vira is like the heart of the apple—"

"The core?" suggests Isabella.

"Yes, she is the core, and I am the skin. She is more inward. I am more outward."

"So, she is introverted and you are extroverted." suggests Isabella.

"Perhaps this is how you can describe it," he says. "I am more confident; she is the careful one. For her it is music and art, for me it is logic and calculation."

"So, you complement each other."

"But also, we are the same in how we think about things."

"Like what?"

He shrugs. "Family, love, religion, politics, food, things like this."

She is watching him closely as he speaks, and she can see flecks of amber in the green of his irises.

He says, "This afternoon, I was confused. I did not know who you were, and I thought there must be some mix-up when we were suddenly," he pauses, choosing his word, "close. But I hoped still it was not a mistake."

Keeping her eyes on his, Isabella says, "When your sister was pretending to be you, it began with the connection I felt through the music. But it wasn't only that. It was also these extraordinary green eyes that you share with her, and the way you both move, and speak, and think—the exotic foreignness of you both. I was drawn in, as you described it, but that Sevastyan always pushed me away." She looks away from him, feeling exposed and vulnerable as she edges towards the crux of all the emotions that got jostled together this afternoon. "When you didn't push me away this afternoon, it was as if—oh, I don't know—as if the final note had been added to change a discord to a resolution. And now, sitting here with you," she turns to him again, "I feel as if I've just leapfrogged over all the bits about getting to know you, and I know you already."

He looks at her, his grin spreading to his eyes. "This is not fair," he says. "You must help me ... what did you say—leap frog? ... so I can know you, too."

She smiles back. "What do you want to know?"

He considers this. "I want to know a lot of things," he says, "but I think what is most important for you is music, so tell me about that."

"It *used* to be the most important thing—too important. It was my whole life. I didn't care about anything else, or anyone else. I was driven, and single-minded, and I think it made me selfish. My brother's death showed me that." She can't believe she is speaking out loud these thoughts that have haunted her, grinding around and around inside her mind for months. She presses on. "I loved him with all my heart, but I still put my career before him, so I didn't get to see him one last time before he died, and it broke my heart. It's why I can't sing anymore, why I won't do Orson's opera."

"But even if you do not sing," says Sevastyan, "it will not change what happened. It is like punishment that has no use. You cannot bring your brother back by not singing."

"But it's the thing that made me a bad person."

"It did not make you a bad person. Maybe you made bad choices, but that does not make you or your singing bad."

She longs to be able to reach out and grab onto this pass that

Sevastyan is offering her. It would ease her guilt for her unconscionable behavior. But she knows that it is a weakness, the human instinct to wriggle out from underneath something that makes you feel wretched. She has to do her due penance for having put herself and her career so egregiously before Julian and his illness. She says nothing.

"If your brother was still alive, is this what he would want?" asks Sevastyan.

The question brings her up short. Julian, who never missed an opening night until the cancer treatment made him too weak to travel. Julian, who kept every program, review, newspaper clipping, and online reference relating to her. Julian, who was her greatest champion, prouder of her than she could ever have been for herself. Her throat starts to ache. She closes her eyes, knowing that the tears will come anyway, but trying to hold them back. In all her grief and self-reproach at not seeing him that one last time, it had never occurred to her that the thing he would most have wanted was for her to continue to try to be the best singer she could possibly be.

She feels Sevastyan's hand warm on her arm. "Is it?" he asks again.

She shakes her head.

"Then must you not sing for him?"

VIRA

WHEN SEVASTYAN HAD ASKED HER with his eyes if it was okay for him to go with Isabella, Vira could tell that he was torn—wanting to stay with her, but also drawn to Isabella. She would have the rest of her life with Sevastyan, but she had no idea when or if they might ever see Isabella and Orson after they left here. So, she gave him her trust to help clear up the messy misunderstandings about her deception. She pulls a deep breath into her lungs. It will also give her a chance to speak to Orson alone, to try to explain.

She watches Sevastyan follow Isabella out of the room, keeping her eyes fixed on the doorway, hearing snatches of unintelligible conversation between Mía and António in the kitchen, acutely aware that she is alone in the room with Orson now—exposed, awkward in their drastically shifted relationship to one another.

"Vira."

He says her name as if he is trying out a new phrase of music.

She looks across the room at him, expecting to see one of his dark moods written all over his face, but finding instead ... she can't explain the look on his face. It's one she hasn't seen before.

"Who are you, really?" he asks.

"I am Vira Blyzinskyj, and I am refugee—"

"Those are the facts I could figure out for myself," he interrupts. "They're just the notes on the page. I want you to give me the musical phrasing. Who are you *really?*"

How typical of him to press deeper for an answer that she can't even fully give to herself. She fills her lungs again. "I look like Sevastyan, and I said I was Sevastyan, but I could not *be* him. You know who I am, really."

"Why didn't you trust me?"

"When I wanted to, it was too late."

He ponders this for a moment.

"So, when you told me that story about your friend who had a secret, and the longer she held onto it the bigger it got, but she just had to keep on doing it, you were talking about yourself?"

He's remembered almost word for word. What else has he stored away in that mind of his?

"Were you?" he persists.

"Yes," she admits. "I wished to tell you, to confess, many times. But you were sometimes..." she tries to think of the word, "in bad mood. I thought maybe you will send me away, and I did not want to go away from your music, or—" She stops herself before she says "you."

"You think so little of me?"

"No! But you would be right to be angry with me for not being honest with you."

Orson stands up, and abruptly sits down again, bouncing one leg up and down. "Surely you could tell how much I liked your company, and respected your musicianship and your insights and your help. Why would I have sent all that away?"

"But you were going to send me away forever this afternoon!"

"That wasn't about you pretending to be Sevastyan! It was about . . . oh, I don't know . . . thinking that you chose Isabella over me."

She takes a moment to absorb this. "Well, it was for me too much risk," she says, "and I was not ready to take this risk. I wanted more time."

"For?"

"For playing your music. For..." She feels as if she is waiting backstage to go on for a performance, as if she is so full of stage fright that she wants to back away, but instead she propels herself forward into the light. "To be with you," she finishes.

"Vira," he says again, softly, as if exploring the feel of it in his mouth. Then, in the same quiet tone, with no more fanfare than if he were giving her directions to his house, he says, "You've fascinated me ever since the first day when I saw you pick up my scattered music and arrange it back in order."

He was fascinated by *her*? When *he* was the one who composed music the way he did, who could coax any sound or dynamic out of the piano, who had so much talent that he didn't know how to accommodate it all in his body, whose mind was constantly thinking and inventing, who was so arresting and magnetic?

"Say something!" he says.

"Orson..." she says. But she is at a loss to try to put anything into words—especially in English.

"Well, at least you've used my name for the first time. That's a start."

"I must speak it in Ukrainian," she says.

"What good will that do me?"

"Let me say it in Ukrainian."

"Okay," he says, on a half laugh. "But speak the way you play music, then at least I stand a chance of understanding."

And so, she begins, her green eyes fixed on his brown ones across the width of the room.

"Я не знаю, коли у мене з'явились до тебе почуття, але, я думаю, це було, коли ми вперше грали твою музику разом." She waits to see if he will respond. He looks baffled.

"It's like nothing I've ever heard before," he says. "But you sounded lyrical, fairly legato, I would say. Tell me what you said!"

She hesitates, then takes the plunge as if immersing herself quickly in frigid water. "I said: 'I do not know when I started to have feelings for you, but I think it was when we played through your music together for the first time.'"

"So, it started a bit later for you."

"But your mood kept changing, and I know you love Isabella—"

"I don't love her."

She stares at him, not trusting herself to believe what she has heard. *Orson doesn't love Isabella?* It shifts the tone of everything, like the sudden modulation from a minor key to a major.

"I don't know when or where those feelings went," he says, "but they're just not there anymore. With you though—" he stops himself. "But finish what you were saying."

It's almost impossible to pick up her train of thought again, but she tries to press on. "Well, to be with you ... it was like playing difficult music that you think you can never know, and then slowly, slowly, it begins to sound under your hands."

"Is *that* how it was for you? It was the exact opposite for me— from the first time you started talking to me about the viol, and playing for me, it felt as if I'd been sharing music with you all my life." He shifts on the chaise longue, as if about to stand, but he stays seated, just staring at her across the breadth of the room.

"Now you know everything," she says at last, "and I don't know what comes next."

When he stands, she does too. She isn't aware that he has moved, but quite suddenly he is standing in front of her. He opens his arms and she walks into them. He pulls her close against his body with his cheek resting on the top of her head. She slides her arms around him, and her hands come to rest on his bony scapulars. She closes her eyes. She can hear his quick breathing and the staccato of his heart. His warm, buttery smell is overlaid with a tang of lemon. *Please*, she thinks, *don't let this moment ever end*.

Instead, it gets better. He threads his fingers through her short hair to tilt her face up to his, and, with the same synchronicity that they have in making music, their mouths come together.

When he tucks her head against his chin again, he speaks into her hair. "I saw what you did with the desk in my room," he says. "It's what you do to me too. You align me, make things more in harmony. I want you to keep on doing it."

She nods against his shoulder.

EPILOGUE

ISABELLA'S APARTMENT IS ABUZZ with musicians and a small, disparate group of audience members. In a simple black shift and low-heeled pumps, Mía glides through the crowd with a tray of light snacks, chatting here, eavesdropping there. It's like her first days of working at Isabella's when there were musical get-togethers almost every other week. Outside, the first snow of the season is falling, hovering like halos around the street lamps, but inside it's cozy and festive in that lull between Christmas and New Year.

"Mía! Over here." Tobia Rutto motions her over to where he is standing with Drew and three other singers. "You mustn't neglect us, *cara*. You remember Drew?" He goes on without waiting for a response, putting a canapé in his mouth and speaking around it. "Meet our Malvolio and Maria and Feste! They will be singing with us tonight."

Mía offers the tray to them, and they juggle snacks with glasses of wine.

Tobia runs his eyes over the crowd, and they alight on Vira. "So, our Sevastyan Blyzinskyj turns out to be a *doppelgänger*, eh? I knew there was something—how do they call it in your country, Drew?—dodgy, no?"

Drew murmurs assent.

"Well," Tobia says, "he or she is a good musician, so we will be forgiving." He sizes up the gathering again. "And the *xenofobo*?" he asks. "Is he here tonight?"

"No." says Mía.

Tobia's eyes light up. "I smell a story here!" he says with the air of someone settling in for a good gossip. "Did you teach him a good lesson?"

"Isabella invited him, but he declined," says Mía. She adds quickly, "Excuse me, but I must go and talk to António."

Tobia snatches another canapé from Mía's tray as she makes her getaway.

António grins at Mía as she approaches. He's brushed off the bartending skills he acquired in Haiti when he worked there to earn enough for the next boat trip en route to the United States. He stands behind the drinks table he's set up in the entrance hall so visitors will be greeted by a welcoming cocktail or a glass of wine.

"I'm using you as an excuse to escape from that man," Mía says to him in Spanish, rolling her eyes towards Tobia. "How's it going?"

"Good," he says. "You want something?"

"No, thanks," she says. "I'm really on my way to the kitchen to pick up more snacks."

As Mía moves off, Fariba Mehta appears on the threshold of the apartment with a dapper man by her side. Fausto has handed over his doorman duties to his nephew for the evening in order to open the door, greet guests, and hang up their coats and hats. Like a magician, he removes Fariba's coat with a flourish that manages to be both urbane and operatic, and he reveals her full-length turquoise sari trimmed with bronze. It lights up the whole entrance hall.

She walks towards the drinks table, smiling. "António, isn't it?" she asks.

"Yes," he says. "Hi again. What can I get you?"

"Sparkling wine, please," she says. "This is my husband, James Bell." She turns to James, whose Brooks Brothers style offsets her exoticism all the more. "This is António Bordones. We referred him to Pascale for an immigration case."

"Ah!" says James. "Pascale knows her way around the immigration system better than anyone. She'll see you right if anybody can."

António breaks into a smile. "Thank you," he says. His eyes move from James to Fariba and he says again, "Thank you."

"We do what we can," says Fariba.

"Can I get you a drink?" António asks James.

"I'll have a bourbon on the rocks, thanks."

When António hands James his drink, Fariba says, "We'd better greet our hostess."

"She's in the music room through there," says António.

They follow his direction into the long, beautiful room with muted lighting and strategically placed candles in sconces that give the space a warm, tawny glow. Pocket doors are opened to an adjacent room where a grand piano, its lid propped open, is grouped with chairs and music stands. About a dozen upholstered chairs have been set up to face what will evidently be the stage area. Through the long windows at the end of the room, snow drifts down against the blackness.

"Fariba!" Peta, looking chic in a dark gray linen pantsuit,

beckons Fariba over to where she is standing with Sevastyan. "I'm glad to see someone else I know," she says. "I was just saying to Sevastyan that this is way out of my milieu. I'm all about oceans and science."

"And for me it is opposite," says Sevastyan. "I grew up with musicians because my father made instruments, and then, of course, Vira. So, when I am busy with quantum computing, I feel sometimes *that* is not really my milieu."

Amidst the laughter, Fariba introduces James.

"But I am glad to be here," says Peta. "It's an honor, really."

"We were looking for our hostess," says Fariba.

"Yes, I haven't met her either," says Peta.

"I will introduce you," says Sevastyan.

Isabella is talking to a couple of the instrumentalists next to one of the candle sconces, and her cloud of blue-black hair is highlighted with a bronze glow. She's wearing a silky, midnight blue sheath. When Sevastyan rests his hand on the small of her back she turns to him, smiling. Then she looks past him.

"You must be the Fariba I've heard so much about," she says.

Fariba glances towards Sevastyan with a smile. "Yes," she says. "This is my husband, James Bell, and I don't think you've met Peta Masters—Vira's host from the Uniting for Ukraine program."

"No, we haven't met," Isabella says, "but I've heard how kind you have been to both Vira and Sevastyan in introducing them to the Ukrainian community."

Peta murmurs how it was her pleasure, and Isabella is in the midst of introducing the musicians to the group when Curtis's voice breaks through the buzz of the crowd.

"Ladies and gentlemen!" he says. "If you'd like to fill your glasses and take your seats, we'll start the proceedings in about five minutes."

Sevastyan leans in to kiss Isabella's cheek, a soft spray of her hair brushing his forehead. "You will be beautiful," he whispers in her ear.

She pulls back, smiling gray eyes meeting green. As she walks towards the stage area, he watches her, as he'd watched her walk away in the darkened auditorium at Peabody when he first met her; then he joins Peta, Fariba, and James making their way to the seating. He picks up the program from his chair and begins to read through it. The cast list is headed by *Olivia — Isabella Foiani*, and listed under the consort, *Vira Blyzinskyj — Bass Viol*.

Isabella is sitting in the row of six chairs alongside the other five singers. In an open semi-circle slightly behind the singers is the consort of six viols, ranging from small to large. The musicians adjust their instruments, re-tuning, playing through a musical phrase here and there. Vira fingers a passage. Her hair has grown out, though she still keeps it short, and she's wearing wide-legged trousers that fall in soft folds on either side of her viol. She looks up, catches Sevastyan's eye, and smiles.

Curtis comes from the back of the room to stand facing the audience.

"Good evening, everyone," he says. "For those of you who don't know me, I'm the director, Curtis Crivello, and I want to thank you all for being guinea pigs for our production before we take it up to the Twelfth Night Festival next week."

Light applause and laughter.

"What you'll be hearing this evening is a concert opera, without costumes and scenery, but I'd like you to imagine an Elizabethan setting, with a few touches from our own time—a ponytail here, a pair of Blundstone boots there—to give it a quirky contemporane-ousness. I'm thinking that most of you, if not all, are familiar with Shakespeare's comedy, *Twelfth Night?*"

Nods and affirmative murmurs.

"Well, what we've done here, in effect, is put together a piece from the outtakes—the comic scenes that don't necessarily revolve around the interplay of love and mistaken identity relating to the four romantic leads. So, it's like a shadow play, if you will, that swings between comedy and pathos." He looks to the back of the room. "Pulling all of it together in musical terms is our extraordinary composer and music director. Please welcome Dr. Orson Carradine." Curtis leads the applause as he moves to sit down in the front row.

Orson is wearing a dark suit and a silk tie with a subtle image of a Medieval illuminated musical score, which Vira found on eBay and presented to him this afternoon. He looks stylish and uncharacteristically well-groomed as he stands, relaxed, in front of the small audience. There is just a hint of the music professor about him as he begins to address them.

"Thank you," he says, "thank you for being here. The whole process of putting together this opera has been so organic that it's fitting to have you as our beta audience, so that you can share your thoughts with us before we take it to the festival next week." He looks over at Isabella, where she sits poised and graceful. "Thank you, Isabella, for hosting us tonight," a smattering of applause, "and most particularly for agreeing to sing my Olivia for me. It was touch and go to persuade you to do it, but it's *your* part, and you are even more stupendous in it than I could have dreamed."

Isabella nods and smiles, but her composure wavers slightly under Orson's lavish praise, and she rests her eyes on the music score in front of her. It's the opening phrase of Olivia's first aria, which Vira, posing as Sevastyan, had described. *It is a woman who mourns her loss. It is music that is sad, but, also in it, there is longing . . . and hope.* Something had touched Isabella's despair on that day, and begun to loosen it—and the more deeply she's delved into the role of Olivia, and identified with her mourning, longing, hope, the more cathartic it has become.

Orson has turned back to the small audience, unaware of the ripple he's caused in Isabella's emotions. "Just to give you a bit of background to the music you'll be hearing this evening," he says, "Curtis mentioned the design, which suggests Shakespeare's era, but with some twenty-first century overlays. This has been my approach to the music, too. I immersed myself in the musical contemporaries of Shakespeare—William Byrd, John Dowland, Robert Johnson, Thomas Tallis, people like this—so that I had their sound in my ear. But I wanted the music to have something of the sonority and tonality of our time, so I've played around with that quite a bit. It won't be hard to listen to, I promise," he says to general laughter. "There's no jarring atonality or anything like that, but don't be surprised by the occasional dissonance—as the plotline suggests from time to time."

He moves from the curve of the piano where he's been standing, and walks around towards the keyboard. "I would never have the gumption to compare myself to Mozart, except in this one particular: I left writing the overture until the last minute." More laughter. "The musicians didn't have a chance to read through it until this morning, and I want to thank the members of the faculty, graduates, and students who have been so generous with their time and skill. They'll be traveling with us to the festival where we will triple the size of the ensemble for the theater up there. For this performance, though, they'll be playing one-on-a-part, so you'll get to hear what superb musicians each and every one of them is."

He sits at the keyboard, and Vira adjusts her position, looking over the opening phrase of the overture to hear it in her mind's ear.

"I would like to single out one musician," says Orson, "Vira Blyzinskyj."

Vira darts a look up at Orson. His eyes, warm and dark, are fixed on her. Her heart starts to thud against the back of her viol.

"Vira plays bass viol," Orson says, "which is the one that looks most like a cello." All eyes are on her. She's overwhelmed by her sudden conspicuousness, and also dazed by what she suspects may be coming.

"If Vira hadn't wandered into my life quite by chance one day and unraveled my composer's block, I think it's fair to say that we wouldn't be playing this opera for you this evening."

The room erupts into applause.

"Vira taught me everything I know about viols and consorts and chests of music from the Elizabethan era," Orson says as the applause begins to subside, "and this would have been a very different work without her."

Orson keeps his eyes on her for a moment, his face gentle, and she is so shot through with a sense of well-being that she has to close her eyes for a second. When she opens them again, Orson has turned to the keyboard, and he plays an A for the consort to tune. As the cacophony of disparate sounds narrows down to a single tone, Vira feels the familiar crackle of expectation in the room.

Briefly, she glances out to where Sevastyan sits between Fariba and Peta, aware as always of his steadying support. And there's something else; something that is new. The trauma of leaving their devastated country is no less real. She still has nightmares about being attacked. She has no idea what shape her future will take after the season at the Twelfth Night Festival. There's talk that the Biden Administration might extend humanitarian parole to Ukrainians for another year, but she and Sevastyan have a precarious status in the U.S. Still, she feels that she has come to rest, for now at least, in this place that was at first so unwelcoming. There's a pulse of possibility, beyond anything she could have imagined when she sat with Sevastyan under the pine tree outside the hospital in Lviv, and felt the first sliver of a wish about coming here.

Vira turns her eyes to Orson again. In stillness, the whole room waits for his downbeat.

Acknowledgements

MY GREATEST ACKNOWLEDGEMENT IS, of course, to William Shakespeare. *Twelfth Night* is probably my favorite of his plays because of the way it blends light and shade, and as an immigrant I empathize with the outsider status of the twins who find themselves strangers in a foreign land. I also love that Shakespeare's own twins, Hamnet and Judith, were his inspiration for the particular bond of siblings. But, this couldn't simply be fan fiction; it was important to tease out the themes of gender and foreignness for their relevance to our time and place.

I gave myself permission to reimagine *Twelfth Night*, because Shakespeare himself had borrowed his themes of cross dressing and mistaken identity from other writers. His earliest source was *Gl'ingannati (The Deceived Ones)*, written collectively by the Accademia degli Intronati in Siena in 1531. Matteo Bandello's *Novelle* (1554–1573), a collection of 214 tales, proved to be a rich source for Shakespeare: *Twelfth Night* drew on story No. 28 from Part II, while *Cymbeline, Much Ado About Nothing,* and *Romeo and Juliet* were also inspired by Bandello's tales. Shakespeare's closest source for *Twelfth Night* was Barnabe Rich, a soldier turned author, who based his 1581 novella *Of Apollonius and Silla* on Matteo Bandello's tale.

Early on in my research for *The Deceived Ones*, I came across the 1591 chalk drawing on paper of *A youth playing the viola da gamba* made by the Bolognese artist, Cesi Bartolomeo. It has been like a talisman throughout my work on the book, which is why I wanted to include it on the cover.

I'm grateful for the generosity of the writing community in Baltimore and beyond. Thank you to Betsy Boyd, Jane Delury, Eric Goodman, Lesley Malin, and Ben Tanzer for their encouragement and kind words, and to Peg Moran for an early edit. Particular thanks to fellow MFA alumna, Danielle Ariano, a beautiful writer and invaluable beta reader, who is always the one to push me further than I thought I could go.

Betty Symington, Director of the Episcopal Refugee and Immigrant Center Alliance (ERICA), sat down with me to explain their important work; how they set about assisting and assimilating refugees and immigrants in the United States. Mark Maarder, American composer, poet, and soldier born in the former Soviet Union, helped me with translations from English into Ukrainian. I'm indebted to both of them for their time and expertise.

Baltimore is a city that grows on you, and it provided the right backdrop for *The Deceived Ones*, because it reflects both light and shade as *Twelfth Night* does. Apprentice House Press, based at Loyola University Maryland, is the perfect publisher for this book set in Baltimore with protagonists inhabiting a university milieu. I am grateful to the Director of the press, Kevin Atticks; acquisitions and copy editor, Abby MacLeod; promotions editor, Maddie Holmes; managing editor and cover designer, Jack Stromberg; and interior designer, Claire Marino. Also to Jessie Glenn, Bryn Kristi, and everyone at Mindbuck Media. Thank you for believing in my manuscript.

Posthumously, my thanks to Peter, who is still with me ten years later, and who taught me everything I know about the unique bond of siblings. And thank you to Douglas, who has had to learn to leave me be for the solitary pursuit of writing, and who supports me in myriad ways.

About the Author

JUDITH KRUMMECK is the author of a memoir in essays, *Beyond the Baobab*, about her immigration from Africa to America, and the biographical memoir, *Old New Worlds*, a finalist in the 2020 Next Generation Indie Book Awards and the 14th Annual National Indie Excellence® Awards. She holds an MFA in Creative Writing & Publishing Arts from the Univeristy of Baltimore, and she is the evening drive-time host for Maryland's classical music station, WBJC.

Apprentice
House Press
Loyola University Maryland

Apprentice House Press is the country's only campus-based, student-staffed book publishing company. Directed by professors and industry professionals, it is a nonprofit activity of the Communication Department at Loyola University Maryland.

Using state-of-the-art technology and an experiential learning model of education, Apprentice House publishes books in untraditional ways. This dual responsibility as publishers and educators creates an unprecedented collaborative environment among faculty and students, while teaching tomorrow's editors, designers, and marketers.

Eclectic and provocative, Apprentice House titles intend to entertain as well as spark dialogue on a variety of topics. Financial contributions to sustain the press's work are welcomed. Contributions are tax deductible to the fullest extent allowed by the IRS.

To learn more about Apprentice House books or to obtain submission guidelines, please visit www.apprenticehouse.com.

Apprentice House Press
Communication Department
Loyola University Maryland
4501 N. Charles Street
Baltimore, MD 21210
Ph: 410-617-5265
info@apprenticehouse.com • www.apprenticehouse.com

Printed in the USA
CPSIA information can be obtained
at www.ICGtesting.com
JSHW010048171223
53780JS00010B/88